A
Harlequin
Romance

OTHER
Harlequin Romances
by JOYCE DINGWELL

THE MUTUAL LOOK

by

JOYCE DINGWELL

HARLEQUIN BOOKS   TORONTO
WINNIPEG

Original hard cover edition published in 1973
by Mills & Boon Limited.

© Joyce Dingwell 1973

SBN 373-01738-3

Harlequin edition published December 1973

Printed in Canada

CHAPTER ONE

THERE was something the matter with Rusty.

Jane was turning this over in her mind as she crossed the final meadow that led to the Little Down Stables. 'Rusty,' she found herself adding ruefully, such a flippant name for the owner of a serious stud. Yet right from the beginning her employer had insisted on that. 'Never call me Mr. Russell,' he had instructed his girl strapper when he had first signed her on five years ago, 'call me Rusty. I had it at school, and it stuck.'

'Yes, Mr.—er—Rusty,' Jane remembered agreeing a little awkwardly on that initial occasion, for to her Rusty had sounded more like one of his chestnuts. 'I'm Jane Sidney. Jane.' She had smiled and put out her hand.

'Welcome to Little Down, Jane.' Mr. Russell had sealed the new union with a press down of his old, gnarled hand on hers.

Yes, old even then, Jane frowned now, pushing the meadow's kissing gate to the yard that led to the outbuildings. She, Jane, had been just eighteen. How old had Rusty been? She smiled affectionately as she closed the gate behind her, then walked on.

Jane's parents, and she had been thankful for this, had been tolerant over her decision to make horses her career. They themselves had tried herbs, seedlings, bonsai trees, then finally finished up growing coffee in Kenya. Jane's brother followed a honey flow. 'You could say,' her mother had laughed, 'that we're outdoor-obsessed.'

Jane felt she had done well at Little Down, and Rusty never had complained. But this last month she had noticed him giving her sidelong looks, she had heard him clearing his throat as people do when they are going to say something important. His health? she had wondered. Health often

5

diminishes as the years accrue. Or was he selling out? Whatever it was she hoped he would not wait too long to tell her. She would have to make plans for her future, strap somewhere else ... or go out to Kenya ... or join her brother David. She was twenty-three, unmarried, not even engaged. Not now. For a moment her lip quivered, but she did not permit any thoughts on *that*. Only on Rusty. What ticked with old Rusty?

The stud was out of Guildford, one of those breath-takingly lovely settings that Surrey does with such heart-warming frequency. A creek at the end of the rough acre, now three fields behind her, was noisy with running water, trees behind the creek bent back against the sky as they took the wind and so spared Little Down, and, since it was autumn, damson, cigar-leaf and gold were changing the hills from their summer bruise-blue. I love it, thought Jane, and I'll hate to go, but there's something about Rusty, some-thing to do with me, and I must know.

She was outside the neat barns of Little Down now, approving, as she always did, Rusty's meticulous arrange-ment. It was a small stud, the only help beside herself several casuals, but it was perfectly set and perfectly main-tained. It also produced, Jane thought proudly, perfect animals.

On Rusty's orders she had just put Simeon in the western section. It was higher there, and Simeon could look down on the fillies in the smaller field, for Rusty believed in courtship as well as marriage. They had been his actual words. What an adorable old man he was, and how she would hate it if——

She stepped inside the first stable and saw that Alex Russell was there before her, there intentionally by the de-termined set of his now stooped shoulders. So she was to know at last. 'Sit down, young Jane.' The old man indi-cated one of the two stools, taking the other himself. He nodded satisfaction at her equipment, all in good clean order, the arrangement of girths, stirrup leathers, buckle guards. 'You're a rare strapper,' he awarded.

'You're a rare boss,' she awarded back.

'But' ... Rusty paused sensitively ... 'not for long.'

So, thought Jane, here it comes.

'I hoped you'd find out,' Rusty said unhappily. 'I hoped to be spared the telling.'

'Of what?'

'That new motorway, Jane,' he said in a rush.

But Jane found she could not answer in a rush. She said slowly, painfully, 'Oh, Rusty, no!'

She had known about the motorway, everyone around here had, but not the actual location. Nor when. But at this moment Rusty was telling her silently, telling her with sad eyes that here, *right here at Little Down*, was the actual location, and the time close at hand.

'I've had my notice to quit, Jane.' Rusty found words at last.

'Any hope of a stay of procedure?'

'This is the final notice, girl—it's been going on all this year.'

'And you never told me? You carried your burden around by yourself?'

'No need to make two people miserable. Only one, now, as it happens, I have come to terms with it. And no one miserable at all if what I plan comes off ... If you'll only agree.'

'What, Rusty?' Jane asked.

'It seems at eighty-four I'm due for the resting paddock, anyway. Now' ... a laugh ... 'you know my age, Jane. I guess you always wondered.'

'I did,' Jane admitted, 'but not as much as I'm wondering now how a man like you will ever rest.'

'I wondered myself until a month ago when an old friend, and a contemporary from ancient stable days, wrote from Kentucky for me to join him there. I know I'd like that, Jane, soft rain and limestone for a man's last years.'

'Rusty, rain and limestone are for good horses.'

7

'What's good enough for a horse is good enough for me. The letter lifted me up again. I'm not fretting any more. Only' ... a careful pause ... 'about you.'

'Darling, I'm not eighty-four.'

'I know exactly how old you are. I have it on your contract. On your record I have other information, Jane, I have the written report that you're the best stablehand, male or female, a man could ever ask.'

'Thank you.' Jane's cheeks, always Surrey-scarlet, now positively flamed with pride.

'Well,' said Alex Russell briskly, 'enough of the blue ribbons, you can't eat ribbons. As you must gather, Jane, because of the motorway I can't sell out.'

'Not the actual stud,' Jane agreed, 'but the stock? The boys? The girls?' They had always called them that between them; they were, Rusty often had remarked, a pair of softies.

'Yes,' the old man nodded, 'and I intend to, Jane.' A pause. 'But not all.'

'Which ones not?'

'The gems, of course,' Rusty said. He had always called their specials the gems.

'Gretel, San Marco, Ruthven,' nodded Jane.

'Also our couple of D's,' added Rusty, 'Dotsy and Devil May Care.'

'You're leaving out the best D.'

'Oh, come now, girl!'

'I mean it, Rusty, you couldn't exclude Dandy.'

Rusty sighed, shrugged his defeat, then corrected, 'Dotsy, Devil May Care and Dandy.'

Jane smiled gratefully at him. 'What happens to them? Over to Kentucky to the soft rain and limestone?' She smothered an ache at the thought of losing Dandy, but after all, if Rusty was with her boy ...

Rusty looked hard at her and said: 'Over to Australia, Jane.'

Jane winced.

There was a silence in the stable, all the horses were out, the only small noise a little breeze worrying at a splinter of straw. 'Now, Jane girl,' Rusty remonstrated, and there was a concerned note in his voice.

'It's all right, I'm over that,' Jane assured him.

'Are you though? Are you ... well, look here, Jane, are you over it enough to—well, to go there, too?'

'Go where?' Jane stared at him stupidly.

'New South Wales.'

'Why should I ever go there?'

'Because that's where the gems are going, over to New South Wales, Australia, to become part of my nephew's concern.'

'Then I'm sorry about that.' Jane's voice was cold. 'Not about your nephew, I don't know your nephew, but——'

'But Australia,' finished Rusty for her. 'And all because of one man.'

'Well, that's one woman's reaction. This woman's.'

'You're foolish, Jane.'

Jane did not answer.

'You're foolish,' Alex Russell went on, 'because you'll be throwing away a job.'

'I can always get employment.'

'Throwing away a better job,' Rusty said, 'superior employment.' A pause, then: 'Plus one-fifth.'

'What, Rusty?' Again Jane said that.

'I'm sending the gems to Australia, Jane. Three of them leave next week, three later, the first three getting into their quarantine stride while you' ... a pause and then a correction ... 'while the second contingent begin their journey.'

'I'm glad you altered that,' Jane said.

'But must I? Think it over, girl. At least' ... appealingly ... 'hear me out now.'

Jane opened her mouth, closed it again. The old man began to speak.

'William Bower is my sole relative. My sister Alice is dead now, and had only the one child.'

'Bower,' Jane said tightly. 'Not the Bower who had the stud called Bowers in the south of New South Wales?'

'Had and has,' Rusty answered uneasily. He added hopefully, 'Studs must have been in the blood.'

But Jane was not to be diverted. '*That* Bower,' she dismissed.

'Jane——'

'Oh, I know I'm mad to go on like this, I know I'm unfair, but any man who employed a man like——like Rodden proved, well——well, he must be the same himself.'

'It doesn't follow, Jane.

'I think it does. You, for instance. Would you employ me if I was——if I——if——'

'I won't be employing anyone soon,' Alex Russell said factually. 'And that's what's worrying me, Jane, I'm worrying about you.'

'I told you, I'm twenty-three and able.'

'That helps you, girl, but it doesn't help me. I'm fond of you, Jane, so fond I just can't let you go without——well, doing something.'

'That's unnecessary.' Jane's voice was stiff . . . stiff from emotion as well as pride. Dear kind Rusty, she was thinking.

'If it was necessary I wouldn't be begging you to do this.'

'To go to Australia?'

'Also to accept that one-fifth,' Rusty reminded her.

'I don't understand what you're saying. All I understand is you want me to go out there, there of all places, and not only there but to Rodden's particular corner.'

'Perhaps not,' suggested Rusty reasonably. 'I mean it needn't be any more. Young vets change their corners continually. They strive for a place of their own, especially ambitious blokes like Rodden Gair was.'

'You're still asking me to go?'

'Yes, I am asking that. Why not?'

'Why not? Why not?' Jane barely prevented a little sob.

At once the old hand covered hers. Alex Russell let his rest there a while, then he said fairly: 'Yes, why not. It doesn't make William, my nephew the same breed.'

'But you don't know, do you, you don't *know* your nephew.'

'No,' agreed Jane's employer, 'I don't, but after all he's my blood.'

'Part,' she reminded him. 'But' ... taking pity on his concerned old face ... 'I'll still hear you out.'

'Thanks for that at least, girl.' Rusty gave a wry grin and started off again.

'I've written to Chad Ramsay telling him I'll join him,' he said, 'finish my days in the soft rain and limestone of Kentucky like a good horse. The family strain in me urges me to give what's left over to my own breed, Jane. I expect you can understand that.'

'Of course.'

'But not entirely, there's a certain filly I can't get out of my mind, and never will.'

'Dotsy.'

'You and your Dotsy! All of your D's. No, it's Jane Sidney, of course. Girl, I can't let you go like this.'

'I told you——'

'And I'm telling you I want you to have one-fifth of my gems. The telling fifth? Who knows?'

'How do you mean?'

'If a man holds four-fifth of something, mustn't the other fifth be the one in control? Mustn't it, girl?'

'I think you're not sure of your nephew,' Jane suggested.

'As near sure as my memory of my sister can make me,' Rusty defended. 'Alice was fine. No, it's not that—well, not entirely that, it's the gems as well. They need you, Jane. Can you say no now?'

'No,' Jane said to show him.

'No to Gretel, San Marco, Ruthven?'

'To Dotsy and Devil May Care, too.'

'Ah—but to Dandy?'

11

'Dandy,' Jane said, and she felt herself biting her lip.

'See!' Alex Russell pounced triumphantly. 'See, Jane?'

Right from his shaky beginning Dandy had been different from the rest. When he had stumbled up from the turf, the vet, Rusty and Jane frankly had been doubtful.

'No gem here,' Bob Westleigh had regretted of the shivering morsel to his client. 'Well, Rusty, you can't have it every time.'

'Does look more like a bit of junk jewellery than a gem,' Rusty had agreed ... and Jane had started to agree, too, then stopped. Dandy had been looking up at her with soft pleading eyes, and she had looked back. The mutual look, Rusty had called it later.

'I always know where there's a mutual look that it will be all right.'

'What is a mutual look?' she had asked.

'Just something between the two of you and you two only. You looked at that fellow, and knew, didn't you? He looked at you, and knew.'

'Knew he could be something?'

'Knew you could make it come true. Well, it will be quite a job, Jane, he's not very prepossessing, but he's yours to do with what you can.'

It had been a challenge, and Jane had taken it up. She had spent more hours on Dandy than she had spent on any other horse. Not just grooming but careful manipulation, tireless massage, the exercising, when Dandy was ready for it, meticulously planned, assiduously carried out. No horse was ever brushed more, polished more, cosseted more. She remembered Rodden saying when he had come to England from Bowers, Australia, to complete a course, and had called, at William Bower's request, to Little Down to meet Bower's uncle, and, as it had happened, Bower's uncle's girl strapper: 'Silk sheets, Janey?' She had remembered laughing back at Rodden, not thinking he was serious.

She hadn't laughed later.

'Dandy?' Rusty was dangling now. 'Look, Jane,' as Jane

12

did not answer, 'I feel pretty sure of William. I have his photo. Would you like to see it?'

'No.'

'There's a look about him.'

'A mutual one?'

'That takes two people.'

'Oh, Rusty, don't go on like this. At least' ... angrily ... 'talk sense.'

'Right,' Rusty said. He probed in his pocket and brought out some papers. 'First contingent,' he told Jane, 'leaving Thursday week. You've just time for your jabs and your what-have-yous, girl.'

'You mean,' she interpreted, 'five weeks out by sea, fly back again, do it all a second time?' She knew that over twelve thousand miles by air would entail a strain on the horse, and that Rusty would never agree to that.

But—— 'No,' Rusty said. 'Half of each—half air, half water. I reckon it would be the best way for the gems. I plan on them flying Boeing to Singapore and then catching their breath during a week or so at sea to Sydney. Does that make good sense?'

It made good horse sense, everything that Rusty had done concerning Little Down always had made sense, but——

'Nice for them,' Jane said.

'And you?'

'Oh, Rusty!'

'Oh, Jane,' the old man said back.

There was silence a while, then Rusty spoke.

'I'm happy in the thought of Kentucky ... couldn't really be happier. I'm happy about William, too. After all, he's Alice's child. But when a man has spent nearly all his life perfecting something, he can't let it go without some backward glance. Jane girl, can't you see that you are that for me, or I hope you will be.'

'The backward glance?'

'Yes. You'd write to me, write personally about the boys

13

and girls, not—well, not like a stranger would write, even though he's the same blood. I wouldn't feel the amputation, in other words. Now do you understand?'

'Yes, Rusty, but don't you understand how I feel?'

'Not entirely. That Rodden Gair——'

That Rodden Gair. Suddenly stifled, Jane got up from the stool and went to the stable door. Rodden, she was thinking. Rod.

It had been a day rather like this when she had first met him, a shining kind of day. He had come down from London to have lunch with Rusty, pass on his boss's and Rusty's nephew's good wishes, and afterwards had strolled out of the Little Down house.

Into Jane's heart.

Tall, blue-eyed, charming, he had won her at once ... and it had been obvious, and flattering, what she had done to him.

Within two weeks they had been engaged. Everything had been whirlwind, magic, romantic, the quick exuberant way a girl wants such things. Rodden was no laggard lover, he had planned marriage the moment they hit Sydney, which, he had said, would be the beginning of next month.

'Oh no, Rod, Melinda foals next month, only in the middle of it, so we'll have to wait a week or so.'

'Darling, you're not serious?'

'I wouldn't be over any of the others, they're normal breeders, but Melinda——'

'Wants you to hold her hoof?'

'Roddy!'

'Janey,' he mocked.

'Rod, I'm in earnest.'

'And I, Jane, have never been more earnest in all my life. Putting a mare before me, the very idea!' He had made a jest of it, but unmistakably there had been no laughter there.

'But I'm not, Rodden. I'll marry you right now. This very moment.'

14

'Only it happens I don't want it like that. I want a ceremony back home, all the glamour and fuss and——'

'You really mean the hand-outs?' He had told her several times about the Bower generosity when any of its members married.

'Perhaps I do,' Rodden had said unabashed.

Jane had been silent a while, she remembered, then she had pleaded: 'You don't have to leave at that time, you could wait an extra week.'

'I'm going at the date I just said. With you.'

'Rodden, I know I sound unreasonable——'

'You do.'

'But this time it means a lot to Melinda. She's been unlucky before, and Bob Westleigh believes——'

'Spare me from a sentimental vet! I've looked the mare over and she's as strong as the proverbial horse.' Rod had laughed at his wit.

'Only,' Jane had inserted quietly, 'she's not.'

'Then she's expendable, my dear Jane, and old Russell should see to it. You can't run a stud on redundant stock. We don't.'

She had noted that 'we', but not commented on it. 'You have to be sensible, I agree,' she said, 'but surely affection——'

'Can't come into business, Jane. Good lord, what have I here and not known it before? A pony high priestess?'

'I am not!' she snapped.

'I've seen dog women,' Rodden had gone on, 'soppy sentimental females drooling over Fido or Rover or Prince, but I've never encountered the horse variety yet.'

'Rodden, I like horses. You must yourself or you wouldn't have followed your career.'

'It's a sound career, and, I hope, in time a rich one, but never if sob stories fill the page instead of figures.'

'Profitable ones, of course.'

'Of course.'

They had stood looking at each other, neither giving

15

ground. If only Rodden had said: 'Darling, I see your point, so see mine, come with me when I say, I need you,' she would have agreed.

But Rodden's lip had stuck out, he had said instead, 'Pony high priestess. All right, stop and hold Melinda's hoof.'

And he had turned and gone.

She hadn't believed it. She had his ring on her finger, his promise in her heart. She loved him, he loved her.

But a week later a letter had come from William Bower, Rusty's Australian nephew, thanking his uncle for the good wishes his vet had brought back with him from Surrey. And that had been all.

Another week and no letter. A month. Two. Jane had boxed the ring and sent it over. Still no communication. At the end of six months she had known it was the end. Such a silly thing to put Finish to it. And yet——

'Is the door shut, girl?' Rusty had asked once; tactfully the old man had requested no details.

'Yes, Rusty,' she had said.

'Then don't fret. I'm not. You two—well, you had no mutual look.'

'Oh, Rusty, you are a fool!'

'Fool's Gold, that's what I'm calling Golden Girl's foal. Like it?'

Slowly but progressively, and eventually without pain though still with a little bitterness, Jane had emerged from her abyss.

Now, she thought, gazing out of the stable door, it could all happen again, if she went.

'It's a long time ago,' Rusty was intoning, 'he'll be in some smart business of his own, that young fellow.' The old man had guessed her thoughts. 'Anyway, what does it matter, Jane?'

'No matter. It's dead.' She said it truly. 'It's just that it makes me wonder about your William Bower.'

'Look at his photo.'

16

'No.'

'All right, don't look, then, but don't see him with Gair's face until you come face to face with him.'

'Which I won't be doing. No, Rusty, I'm sorry. If you want to—well, reward me, why can't it be without going out there, without giving me a share of the gems? One gem would do,' she said intensely.

'Yes—Dandy. But what would a scrap like you do with Dandy? Especially now that we know——'

'Yes?'

But Rusty had not continued with that. 'Horses cost money, Jane,' he said, 'a deal of money, you should appreciate that. William has enough, I believe, some from his parents, most from his own initiative. If Dandy is to have the best, it's to be out there.'

'Very well' ... a sigh ... 'consign Dandy, too.'

'With you?'

'No, Rusty. It will hurt me terribly, but I would get over it.'

'I wouldn't,' the old man said sadly. 'I'd feel cut off completely from my fellows knowing you weren't there ... well, until they were acclimatized, anyway.'

Jane pricked her ears at that. 'Till they became acclimatized ... then it need only be temporary?'

'I'd like it to be longer, but I haven't made that stipulation.'

'Rusty, just what stipulations have you made?'

He brightened at that, evidently seeing a gleam of hope, and, folding his arms, looked across at her, still standing at the door.

'The stipulations are that to earn that share you must go out and work with our two consignments. When you judge them as properly settled in, when William judges them as that as well, if you like you can sell out your dividend.'

'Oh, I'd do that all right,' she promised.

'Then you'll go, Jane?'

'I haven't said so.'

'If you don't go, then what will you do?'

'Another job ... I told you ... the parents ... or follow the honey with David. He writes that honey is very lucrative.'

'And be happy while you're doing this?'

'Of course.' Her voice was too enthusiastic, and she knew he would pick it up.

He did. 'Transparent Jane,' he said, 'you'd be miserable away from horses, you're a real——'

'Pony high priestess?' she said sharply.

'That Gair!' Rusty fumed. 'He certainly did a bad job.'

'Well, it's done.'

'I don't think so. Not entirely. You know what I think?'

'What, Rusty?'

'I think Dandy will win this argument, that you'll go because of him.'

'No!' Jane declared.

'Then I believe I'll win, that you'll go because of me.'

She had turned right back from the door now and she looked fondly down on the old man.

'You're not really so happy being put out to grass,' she insinuated gently, 'even Kentucky blue grass.'

'No, but I could be nearly happy knowing that Gretel, San Marco, Ruthven——'

'Dotsy, Devil May Care——'

'Dandy,' they both said together.

Rusty finished, 'Were in my girl's hands.'

'Only till I bow out,' she stipulated.

'Yes.'

'And if I can't stand it I can waive that fifth and leave on my own accord?'

'Yes.'

'Then——'

'Then, Jane?'

'I'll do it.'

'Thursday week the first contingent, twelve days to go out by air and ship, two days to fly back and to start it all

18

again. I'll be waving you away on the fifteenth of June, Jane, and should welcome you home the beginning of the next month prior to you going off again.'

'Then Kentucky for you?'

'And Australia for you. Write often, Jane.'

Jane said a little chokily, 'Yes, Boss.'

CHAPTER TWO

ALMOST at once, or so it seemed to a saddened Jane (and no doubt Rusty) the jack hammers began. Men invaded Little Down with all varieties of destructive machines, men looking like invaders from other planets in their yellow safety gear and steel helmets. Bulldozers lumbered in, semi-trailers, salvage lorries, and as they advanced, the stud ceased functioning.

The lesser lights were dealt with first, among them Toby, who had loved apples and actually pulled them from trees, Minnie, who once had bitten a rather pompous VIP visiting Little Down and who still wore a smile of wicked remembrance, Melinda, because of whom Rodden had departed, along with Melinda's several offspring, for one good thing had come out of that episode : Melinda had beaten her birth hoodoo and was now the perfect mare.

Each farewell wrenched Jane. She wondered what Rodden Gair would have had to say about that. She wondered if mindlessness was an Australian trait. If so, what would William Bower have thought?

Because Rusty had been in the habit of sending Jane abroad fairly regularly to pick up some colt or deliver some pony, her shots were up to date. All she had to do was pack and collect her tickets. While collecting, she changed the class from First to Tourist. Dear Rusty, how typical of him to cosset her! Well, he need never know that she had altered her travelling standard, and she was sure he could do with the extra cash.

Saying goodbye was not so hard; she would be back in little more than a fortnight. The thought of saying goodbye the next time, though, made Jane feel bleak.

She, Gretel, San Marco and Ruthven left duly from Gatwick, the mare and two geldings by air freighter, Jane minutes after them by a regular line. The plan was to rest the girl and boys at a Singapore stable owned by an old customer of Rusty's. A day would be sufficient, and a day would fit in admirably with the departure of the *Southern Princess* for Sydney.

The flight to Singapore proved comfortable and uneventful. One quick check of the four-legged travellers assured Jane that Gretel, San Marco and Ruthven had fared just as well.

She had a pleasant stopover in Singapore, doing the usual things ... Bushy Hill, Change Alley, selecting a length of Thai brocade to be made into a cheongsam in one day and delivered to her *Southern Princess* cabin.

It was there when she boarded, and, to her delight, a perfect fit. About to change back, she decided she had better check up on her precious cargo; she had left full instructions for the boarding of the mare and geldings, but she had not actually seen them on the ship. Running along the narrow passage of her tourist class deck, she giggled to herself at her unworkmanlike gear. She must be the oddest pony high priestess ... she never forgot that from Rodden ... in the world.

No one saw her, however, and she gained the appropriate deck without attracting any stares. She slipped past several boxes of unenthusiastic canine travellers, stopped to cheer up a disapproving white cat on a leash, then found the girl and the boys. Well, they were there all right, but not, she saw at once, very happy.

She checked their tethering—it was not too tight—she saw to water, availability of movement, light, several other necessary details. It was while she was attendding to a small leg cut that Ruthven must have suffered in transit that she noticed a foot among the hooves. A man's foot. A long, expensive-looking shoe in dark tan leather. Dark tan socks above it. The end of a dark brown trouser leg.

She looked up.

The horses' berth was exclusively their own, this was

21

something she had not changed when she had changed her standard of travel. Which made this man an intruder.

'Did you want something?' she asked sharply.

'No.' That was all he said.

'Then I must ask you to leave.'

'Not before I ask you to tie those horses in the other direction ... that is if it's your job.'

'It is.'

'I'm surprised. Since when have strappers worn brocade?'

'It's a cheongsam I bought in——' Jane stopped in annoyance, annoyed at herself. What did it have to do with this man? 'You're trespassing,' she said instead.

'I'm leaving at once. I merely stopped to look at the ship's arrangement, see what quarters they offered.'

'If you've seen, will you please go?' she demanded.

'Not before you change that tethering.'

'Why should I?'

'Because,' he fairly burst out, 'the beasts are uncomfortable. For heaven's sake, can't you see that?'

Jane looked and saw that obviously they were, though why they should be she did not know.

'We're *sailing*, in case that fact hasn't reached you,' the man said, 'and the way they're tied, they're getting more than they should of the not inconsiderable swell. But perhaps pony high priestesses' ... pony high priestesses? ... 'are unaware that a horse can be seasick. I assure you they can be quite dangerously so, dangerous because they don't possess the therapy of being able to retch.'

She knew all that, Rusty had instructed her, but she still could not find words to defend herself. *Pony high priestess*, he had said.

And then something was pushing aside Jane's wonder, her resentment. The ship was certainly moving, indeed, down here, moving quite unpleasantly. To her utter dismay and to the ruin of her new cheongsam, *Jane* was now being sick. Thoroughly sick. At once the man tossed across an overall,

22

and while she pulled it on he moved over to her, then propelled her to the door.

'I'll change them around for you,' he said briefly. He took time to look her up and down. 'I don't know whether that stuff cleans,' he added, 'but if it doesn't you can discard the soil and use the rest as rags. You always want rags.'

She hated him for that, hated him for seeing her sick, for commenting on her now poor bedraggled little cheongsam, in short she simply hated him. Leaving the girl and boys in his hands, something a really responsible strapper would never do, ill or not, Jane ran back to her berth.

Once away from the horses' quarters she felt much better. She regained her cabin, was relieved to find it empty, undressed, wrapped up the cheongsam distastefully and put it aside for disposal whenever convenient, then showered and put on fresh clothes.

The chance to throw away the offending garment came at afternoon tea time. Instead of obeying the gong as the rest of the tourist class appeared to be doing, Jane hurried back to her cabin and picked up her parcel, regretting as she did so that her economy on account of Rusty had deprived her of a porthole; a porthole would have been very convenient just now.

When she went up on deck it was to apparent emptiness. She lost no time in hurrying to a strategic position ... only to be beaten to the chosen spot in a very unnerving fashion. Two figures ... in her confusion at first Jane did not see they were children ... had run forward and before her horrified eyes were toppling over a figure. She could not see any details, but she sensed hair hanging down, a hat of sorts on top of the hair.

'Stop at once ... what have you done ... Steward! Purser! Cap——' The last she uttered to the accompaniment of peals of laughter. Looking down to the sea she saw an old mop riding the waves.

'You little fiends!' She realized now that the pair were quite young.

23

As they still doubled up in mirth, she threw away her own evidence, then, relieved on two counts, one that murder had not been done, two that she had rid herself of the wretched cheongsam, Jane joined the laughter. She and David had staged larks like this, and anyway, she liked children.

They seemed a little surprised at her participation, and looked at her with interest. Jane found herself looking back at them with equal interest. Twins undoubtedly, male and female version, but like as proverbial two peas.

'Robert and Roberta,' they introduced themselves.

'Jane,' said Jane.

'Where are the rest of the people?' they asked.

'Afternoon tea. Don't you pair like cakes?'

'We're First,' they said unenthusiastically, 'and the only kids in First this trip. It's awful in First, just like a morgue. In Tourist you have a ball. Are you having a ball?'

'I only boarded at Singapore.'

'So did we, but we sailed up. It was just as bad then. Why can't Father William book Tourist instead?'

That had been Roberta, identical with Robert as to basin-cropped hair, sloppy joe, shorts and sandals, but slightly smaller and finer in build.

'Because,' explained Robert, 'there are nine hundred Tourists but only a hundred Firsts, so Father William reckons there's all that less for us to drive mad.'

'Do you drive people mad?' Jane asked.

'Yes,' they said factually, 'we're indirigibles.'

'Do you mean individuals or incorrigibles?'

They could not remember, but they were agreed that it was something bad.

'We have a bad name,' Roberta said.

'That's true, and it's probably deserved.' This was Robert, more articulate than his twin. 'You see, we're unsettled. Our mother is doing a course in Paris, so Father William has to have us until we can go on to school. He's not very happy.'

24

'But,' came in Roberta, 'he's going to be unhappier still.'
They both went into peals of laughter again.

'Show her,' Roberta urged Robert.

'She could tell.'

'No, she's all right. She laughed about the body. Besides, she won't see Father William down here in Tourist, so she can't tell.' Roberta looked at Jane. 'You wouldn't tell, anyway, would you?'

'I would tell about a real body, anything like that.'

'It isn't, it's a passport—Father William's passport. We've put a photo over his photo. Wait till he has to show it!' They doubled up again.

On Roberta's prompting, Robert took out the passport. 'It's all right,' he reassured an alarmed Jane, 'I take good care of it. Look.' He showed her the usual document, only where the likeness should be, a likeness ... if such a likeness could be like to anything ... of something else.

'It's an artist's impression of the Yeti, the Abominable Snowman,' Robert said proudly.

Jane tried to look severe, but the dripping whiskers and long black teeth undid her. Again she laughed.

'See,' the pair rejoiced, 'she's one of us. Why aren't you in First?'

'The usual reason,' Jane said, wiping her eyes. 'And after this' ... looking at the passport now being carefully returned to Robert's pocket ... 'I can't say I want to better myself. You two are——'

'Robert! Roberta!' The summons came from a deck above, the deck of the more exclusive section of the ship. It was a man's authoritative voice. Jane had no time to see the caller, but she did see the reaction of the children. They might be individuals or incorrigibles, but, as far as that voice was concerned, they were disciplined.

'Blimey,' they said together, and turned and obeyed their summons without another word.

The episode had cheered Jane. Giggling over the Abominable Snowman, she went down to look at her girl and

25

boys again, much more suitably clad this time, she thought, wondering if she would encounter that man again. She supposed she would have to thank him. That would be hard. It could never be easy apologizing to someone who had seen you being most unglamorously ill. However, there was no one about, the stable occupants looked fit and settled, so Jane came out again. As she crossed to her deck to relax in the sun, she saw the twins on the deck above her. They caught sight of her and waved enthusiastically, and Jane waved back. If she encountered them again, she thought, she must ask why they said Father William of their parent, that parent who had the care of them while their mother did some course in Paris, and who was not very happy over it, or so they had said. Jane found a chair, turned over the pages of a magazine ... Slept.

She saw the twins fairly frequently in the shipboard days that followed. Whenever they could escape to Tourist, they did so, and after a charity concert in the First Saloon open to all who cared to donate, Jane did not blame the small people. Luxury to children could never take the place of companionship, contemporary companionship, and the only people she saw in First were distinctly mature. Across the room she glimpsed the man who had trespassed into the stable berth during her primary check there. She was not surprised to find him here, not someone with an autocratic look like he wore. If he noticed her, he made no sign. Jane gave her attention to the music ... yet not entirely as before. Oddly uncomfortable, she was glad when it was time to return to the stern.

Whenever they could the twins would sneak down and look longingly at the pool.

'You have a pool of your own,' Jane reminded them. 'A much better pool.'

'Inside, in case the poor old dears get sunburned,' sneered Roberta.

'Anyway, no one goes in, except Father William, so

where's the fun?' Robert looked jealously at a boy ducking a girl.

'Why do you call him that? Father William?' Jane asked curiously.

'William's his name, and once he said he'd kick Robert downstairs.' It was Roberta, and she reported it in a suitably scandalized voice, but Jane gave a tolerant smile and asked: 'What had Robert done?'

'Nothing at all. Only put a bucket of water where Father William would tread into it, but he didn't,' said Robert.

'Then no wonder he was angry. I would have been, too. Why do you do such things?'

'Childish exuberance,' they both proffered together, and when Jane refused to accept that, they defended, 'Our mother says so, anyway.'

'It's plain naughtiness,' Jane scolded. To change the subject she said: 'Lewis Carroll wrote *Father William*. Did you know he wrote *Alice in Wonderland* as well?'

'Oh, I like Alice. Remember the part where she finds the little cake with EAT ME in currants?' It was Roberta.

'Yes, and that part——' took up Robert.

Jane knew, and participated. When they had to leave they said wistfully, 'You're fun, Jane.'

She did not see the twins for several days, in fact they had left Malaysia behind and when sailing down the west coast of Australia to Fremantle before the pair descended on her again.

'We've been in bad trouble,' they sighed.

'What did you do?'

'You saw it.'

'Not the photo?'

'Yes. Father William had to take it when he went ashore at Djakarta. We were to go with him in the afternoon for a tour.' A sigh. 'We never went.'

Jane tried hard to keep a straight face. She could imagine the effect of the Abominable Snowman looking up through his dripping whiskers to the officer at Passport Control.

27

'You awful children!' she said ... then broke down.

The Australian Bight, several days later, lived up to its reputation and proved quite rough. Jane spent most of her time with Gretel, San Marco and Ruthven. They plainly did not care for the motion, but they weathered it fairly well. Jane did not care for it, either, not down there, but she weathered it, too.

Then Adelaide was taking them into its calmer waters, and after Adelaide, Port Phillip Bay, fortunately in a benevolent mood, and soon they were steaming up the New South Wales coast. They came into Sydney on a bright blue and gold day, journey's end for Jane's girl and boys, but not yet for Jane herself.

She looked to the upper First-Class deck in the hope of seeing the twins, saying goodbye to them, for she had become very fond of the naughty little pair. They were not in sight, but the autocrat was. He returned Jane's look with an equal look, and that, shrugged Jane, was putting it in precisely the right words.

She did not encounter the children again, even if she had she would not have found the time to talk with them. Until she left Kingsford Smith Terminal for the U.K. once more, she had not a minute to spare. She settled the horses in quarantine, stopped with them as long as she was permitted, then spent the rest of her hours to her departure wondering whether she should ring up Rusty's nephew ... she had looked at a map and seen that the place was too far away for a casual visit ... then gave the thought away and took in a few city highlights instead. In no time she was aboard a Jumbo and speeding home. Home, she mused. I must get out of saying that. I don't know how long it will take once all the boys and girls get to Bowers for them to settle, but I should think it would be a fair part of a year.

This time it was hard to part from Rusty, they both made light of it, but there were sudden breaks in the laughter, and Rusty's hand holding hers was tight.

'Keep me posted, Jane.'

'Everything, Rusty ... including Dotsy's colt or filly if we mate her out there, for I feel she should begin, don't you?'

Rusty mumbled something indecipherable, and Jane put the mumble down to distress. He was distressed, the poor old dear. 'They tell me there's no grass like Kentucky blue,' she cheered him as they left.

Again she went over the previous programme ... checked the three D's, Dotsy, Devil May Care and Dandy at Singapore ... saw to their embarkation this time to the *Ariadne*.

The second sea trip began. Right from the start it was much more pleasant, the company was more her own age and outlook, and, though she still missed the twins, there was John.

She liked John Rivers at once. In the way people pair up in ships, she found herself pairing instinctively with the young man. They took shore excursions together, John altered his table in the dining saloon to be with her.

After a strenuous deck tennis bout one day, John said: 'I know all about you *now*, but nothing about you *yesterday*, and what's more important, nothing about you *tomorrow*.'

'That's easy,' she laughed. 'I was a strapper ... the same as I am now, and incidentally, John, Devil May Care is looking quite devilish again.' The horse had been slightly off colour.

'And tomorrow?' John smiled; he had a pleasant boyish smile.

'Strapper, or stablehand, once more. Place called Plateau in New South Wales. Would you——' She had started to ask 'Would you know it?' but saw at once that he did. He was beaming at her, crinkling his nice bramble-brown eyes in pleasure.

'Of course I know it. In fact I'm only some twenty miles away in the valley. We'll be neighbours, Jane.'

Jane crinkled her own eyes back. She felt as pleased as he obviously did. 'It's going to make it much easier,' she appreciated, 'knowing you're there.'

'For me, it's going to make it——' But John reddened and did not finish.

A little embarrassed, Jane said, 'Tell me about this place.'

'You mean you don't know anything about where you're going?'

'I don't.'

'Then,' he smiled, 'I'll tell you. You're going to perhaps the loveliest corner in the world.'

'That's local pride.'

'I expect so, but it's still a glorious spot. It's in the south ... can get quite cool in winter ... beautiful timber as well as good pickings for hops.'

'Which are you, John, trees or hops?'

'Some of both, and doing nicely, thank you, though never, of course, as well as the Baron of Bowers.'

'Why do you call him that?'

'He looks a proud devil, though I'm assured he's quite a decent guy. Severe, perhaps, but then you have to be when your commodity is livestock—I mean, Jane, I love trees, but they're still not flesh and blood.'

'And hops, do you love hops?'

They both laughed at that, then John went on to tell her more about the place.

'The district is called Urara, which is aboriginal for Far Away. I suppose it was far away once, but these days of air travel——'

'There's facility for landing, then?'

'At Plateau, private only. That's where Bowers is situated. I'm down the valley, so I take the official coastal route if I fly. But I won't be flying this time, I'll be trucking it, and I hope you'll come with me.'

'By truck?'

'Yes, Jane. Too lowly?'

'It's just wonderful,' Jane enthused. 'In that way I'll see the country.'

'Then that's fine,' John smiled.

The days sped fast, the weather was kind, the horses never looked back, and in no time the red roofs of Sydney were looming up again.

'You'll have to give me a day to settle Dotsy, Devil May Care and Dandy,' Jane stipulated to John Rivers.

'I'll wait a year if you say so,' John said deliberately.

She did not answer that, but she was not unpleased.

But Jane spent no day settling her trio. The moment the *Ariadne* berthed, a figure she would have recalled, had she been on deck to watch, joined the ship, joined it in that confident manner confident men always do. But Jane was not there.

She was putting last things into her case when the message came over the loudspeaker.

'Wanted at once at the Purser's Office: Miss Sidney. Wanted at once by Mr. Bower: Miss Sidney.'

Jane was halfway there before that 'at once' struck her, and then she fumed. She had barely arrived, she was not in anyone's employment yet, how dared he . . .

She came to the office, then stopped short. It could be only coincidence, but there appeared to be no one else here, apart from the uniformed purser, than——

'Miss Sidney, I presume.'

He wore country corduroys this time, a rather wide-brimmed hat, but there was no mistaking the identity of that man who had tossed her an overall in the *Southern Princess*, who had impelled her outside to be sick.

'Mr. Bower?' Jane asked faintly.

He said: 'Yes.'

'Are you packed?' William Bower inquired briskly.

Jane nodded.

'Good, then. I'm hoping I can get you a quick passage through Customs.' But his tone did not evince mere hope, it evinced haughty confidence. 'Then we can make a prompt start.'

'Start to where?'

31

'To Bowers, of course.'

'Urara.'

'I see you know the name.'

'John told me.' Jane added, 'John Rivers.' As there was no comment, she added again: 'He knows you.'

'A lot of people in the game do.'

'He's not in the game, if you mean the stud game. He grows hops and raises timber in Urara.'

'Interesting.' He said it in an uninterested voice. 'He'd be in the valley, then. Bowers is on the plateau, which very originally' ... he did not accompany it with a smile ... 'is called Plateau.'

'And the stud is called after you, of course.'

'A mere coincidence. I really named it after the bower-birds that are there.'

'Still there? Hasn't the activity of stables moved them on?'

'Bower-birds don't move on, they simply make a bower and then commute there from their nest. Sometimes it goes on for their lifetime. You said you were ready?'

'No. That is ... I mean there's John.'

'Yes, you mentioned him.' William Bower waited.

'I'd said I would travel down with him.'

'To Urara?'

'Yes.'

'Why the devil would you say that?' He glared at her.

'Why shouldn't I?' She glared back.

'Because during my employment of you——'

'You're forgetting that I'm in a slightly different category from the usual employee.'

'Ah, I'd expected this.' William Bower pushed the wider-brimmed hat than usual, a hat he had not taken off yet, to the back of his head. 'My uncle couldn't have made a more idiotic arrangement if he'd tried.'

'I have no doubt that he did try,' she said coldly.

'On your persuasion?'

'If you're referring to that one-fifth——'

32

'What else?'

'I had nothing to do with it.'

'But plenty to do with it now,' he suggested.

'No. I mean——' She stopped. How could she say to this unapproachable man that the final and *telling* point of Rusty's 'idiotic arrangement', as William Bower expressed it, had been the loving fact of Rusty himself?

'I think you might be under some misapprehension, Miss Sidney.' The man was packing a pipe and lighting it. 'You have that one-fifth all right, for what it's worth, but it's more bonus than status. I really mean to say that it comes *because* of your employment under a new boss, not *with* it. In short, employment and not a directive capacity.'

'Bonus.' Jane repeated his word.

'That's what I said.'

'But' ... a pause from Jane now ... 'still—a telling bonus?'

'You have one-fifth of the stock that have come from U.K. Note that, please, the U.K. fellows only. Taking in their consignment costs, their quarantine costs, a million and one other costs, at present that one-fifth means nothing at all—indeed, you're well in debt. But my uncle must have considered all this, for he added the stipulation of your employment. Under me. You are employed right now, and the steep way charges soar in this country you should be glad of this. So' ... a shrug ... 'start earning your money.'

Jane had flushed vividly. 'I didn't intend not to. I meant to settle the new lot, check up on the old, then——'

'And then jaunt down with Rivers? No need for any of that. I've seen to the first three fellows, made arrangements for the next three, so we can get away at once.' He added, 'By air.'

'John is going by road.'

'Unless he flies to Ribberton on the coast, the only other way, there's no rail there.'

She was disappointed, she had looked forward to seeing the country down to Urara. She knew John would be dis-

33

appointed, too.

'Have you booked for me?' she asked hopefully, hopeful that he might not have done so, might try now and be unsuccessful.

'I fly my own craft,' he said shortly.

'Then' ... inadequately ... 'at least I must tell John.'

'Oh yes, certainly tell him.' Before she could move, he moved to the desk, and the next moment Jane heard: 'Wanted at the Purser's Office, Mr. Rivers.'

What an autocrat this man was! Yet ... seeing John already down the passage ... what a successful one!

But when the valley man joined them, Bowers treated him amiably. They talked together for a while on Urara. William Bowers asked him if he would like an air lift down.

'There's room,' he assured him, 'it's a specially constructed craft in case I ever have to fly up a patient, and I don't think' ... a grin ... 'you're bulkier than a horse.'

'That's kind of you, but I have my own transport.' For a moment John looked wistfully at Jane. 'I brought the lorry up to Sydney, then left it here because I knew I would need it on my return. I made quite a few machinery purchases in Singapore.'

'Then we'll leave you. Please call in to Bowers should you feel like it. I know we have rather different interests' ... the slightest of pauses and the slightest of glances at Jane ... 'but you may find it a diversion.'

'Thank you, I will come. Goodbye, Jane.'

'Goodbye, John.' Jane did not put out her hand, she just smiled ... though she felt more like pulling a wry face.

As William Bowers had said, customs was soon dealt with, so evidently the 'Baron' had influence. They emerged from the wharf and Bowers hailed a taxi. 'Stock quarantine,' he directed the driver.

Jane looked at him in surprise. 'I thought we were leaving for Bowers immediately.'

'Immediately after you check your bunch.'

'I thought you checked them.'

'Only my four-fifths of them.' He said it coolly, but the fact that he was giving her the opportunity to see Gretel, San Marco and Ruthven before she went south impelled Jane to thank him.

For a moment he looked at her without the lift of one sardonic eyebrow, a habit, she had noticed, of his whenever he had something pertinent to say, which seemed most often. 'Like them, don't you?'

'Oh yes.'

'Is that—good?'

'How do you mean, Mr. Bower?'

'I mean' ... he said deliberately as he repacked his pipe ... 'Rodden Gair.'

'Oh——' Jane exclaimed. 'He's still with you?' she asked presently.

'No.'

'Then can—can we *not* talk about it?'

'It would bore me if you did,' he replied, and made no further exchange. After a while he indicated: 'Here is Sydney quarantine, sea view and all. I think you'll find your boys and girls are quite happy in their temporary quarters. Why are you looking at me like that?'

'Boys and girls. Rusty and I always said that.'

He did not reply, but she saw that he reddened.

'How long will Gretel, San Marco and Ruthven be?' she inquired.

'They've nearly finished their term. This next lot——'

'Why, they're here already!' Jane explained in surprise and delight. Now she would be able to say 'Goodbye, it won't be long' to Dandy. 'You certainly get things done, Mr. Bower.'

'I need to, when they get done to me.' He opened the door for her and she stepped out. She felt like answering him in his own coin, but at least he had availed her Dandy. She went across to where a float was discharging a load of three, touched two satin heads in turn ... and nuzzled a grey one. Dandy's.

The man waited for her. At last Jane turned and said, 'Thank you, I'll come now.'

He nodded and they returned to the taxi. They did not drive to Kingsford Smith where Jane had boarded a Jumbo back to England but to Bankstown where the private craft put down.

Waiting in a corner of the field was a light plane that William Bower claimed as his, a neat but capacious Cessna, custom-built, he told her. 'Made for my special needs, Miss Sidney. Climb in.'

Jane obeyed. They took off smoothly, circled the field, then set off in what he called out was a south-south-west direction. 'We don't cross the Divide,' he went on, 'only land on it when we reach Plateau on the plateau.'

They were passing over countryside now, their craft travelling in shadow on the green-gold fields beneath. Bush followed, olive-green terrain, but lit up here and there by warm yellow that the man beside her told Jane was wattle. To the right, he indicated the mountains of the Great Dividing Range, jutting pinnacles straining upwards, yet evidently not so lofty as many mountains rate, for every peak wore a crown of trees. Fascinated, Jane looked down, traced streams beneath that ended in silvery ribbons of waterfalls, traced clearings where some hardy soul had carved out a farm. Then, without any warning, a wide pasture, a golden summit that spread out lushly on four sides but was stopped by cliff edges on each of the sides, looked back at her, an oasis of neat paddocks, of perfectly symmetrical buildings imposed on the paddocks, everything as clear-cut and disciplined as in a child's farmyard set. 'Urara Plateau,' the pilot called. Then he added with pride: 'Bowers.'

No wonder he was proud, Jane thought unwillingly but honestly as she got down on a field as neatly clipped as a suburban lawn. No old thistle here, tousled bramble, sloe, just immaculately shaven grass.

A jeep was coming out for them; on its side was inscribed 'Bowers', then a bower-bird, rather the shape of a Bird of Paradise, Jane thought, imposed.

'Is he like that?' she asked of the sign.

'Yes, he's a relative of the Paradise chap. You'll see him. Hi there, Jake.' The jeep had pulled up. 'This is Jake, Miss Sidney.'

Jane smiled and the man grinned back. The bags were stowed and the jeep started the run to the model buildings she had looked down on from the Cessna.

Often, Jane thought a little spitefully, things look better from a distance, so perhaps the stud...

No, it was perfect, quite perfect, Rusty should have seen it. She said it aloud.

'I'd have liked the old man to have come out, but he had different ideas.' A small pause. 'What was Little Down like?'

'Beautiful, but not in this way. We were small.' She saw him noticing that 'we' and tightening his lips.

'I' ... a slight emphasis ... 'am large, as you will soon see. The quarters, please, Jake. Miss Sidney will want to settle in, she can tour later.' The jeep came to a halt in front of a large red-brick building. 'It's laid out in motel style,' William Bower informed her, 'and is serviced, Miss Sidney, so don't waste any time on domestic chores. You'll find the women's quarters are to the right, the men's to the left. Separated,' the man added, 'by the canteen, an all-hours canteen, so no need to knock off to get in for a meal for fear it will go off. Jake will carry up your bags.'

Jake did carry them, and Jane followed Jake. She did not turn round to see what William Bower was doing, she knew he would still be sitting in the jeep watching her. But at the door curiosity overcame resolution, and she did turn to look.

The man looked back.

The motel, for it could have been that in layout, was two-storeyed. 'Twenty mod bedrooms,' Jake, carrying the bags and leading the way, told Jane, 'all singles, all with built-ins, television, own bath recesses.

'Then there's two big rec rooms and two laundries, though the room linen, of course, is done for Bower's boys.'

'And girls?' Jane had been wondering if there would be female strappers as well as herself.

'Girls, too, even the married couples, though they're not in the motel but in flats across the way. If you don't feel like going down for a cuppa, Miss Sidney, there's always provision in your room.' They had reached the room by now, a generous sixteen by sixteen with all that Jake had boasted, as well as a snack corner providing milk, sugar, tea, a packet of biscuits, a few tinned easy meals.

'He doesn't appear to have forgotten anything,' said Jane.

'Not him,' admired Jake.

'Where will I find the work roster?'

'Reckon you'll be written down on it?' Jake doubted. 'I'd rather gathered you weren't exactly the usual stable-hand.'

'I'm in Mr. Bower's employ,' said Jane factually. What had the Baron said to her? 'That fifth say is more bonus than status . . . it becomes *because* of your employment, not *with* it.' Then: 'Employment and not a directive capacity.'

'Reckon I'll be down.' Jane adopted Jake's manner of speech. They grinned at each other.

When he had gone she looked around her. The room was very tasteful, she found. Instead of the mannish tans she rather expected in a strapper's quarters, male or female, everything leaned to a soft woodsy green. It made for a more feminine touch as well as suited the pleateau setting.

She went to the window and looked out. The view was magnificent. No mountains, for they were on the mountains, but rolling pasture as far as the eye could see, and that, Jane knew from her Cessna lookout, was where the cliffs, four sides of them, dipped down to four surrounding valleys.

She noted the immaculate lawn verges between each row

of buildings, a garden with tended plots and a shrubbery. Further to the right was a large single-storeyed house enclosed from the rest of the estate. *His* house, she thought. A rotary clothes line was idling round in the warm breeze. She saw some smallish jeans hanging from it, two pairs of them, two pullovers. Children's. So the Baron was a family man. She wondered, idly like that idle wind, about his wife.

Though she was tempted to brew some tea in the privacy of her own room, she knew that this was never a way to settle in. She brushed her hair, rubbed in a suggestion of lipstick, all the make-up she had needed in the crisp air of Surrey, then went down to the canteen. A cook in full equipment greeted her genially and asked her to name it.

'Just a cuppa,' she said, laughing. 'I know I could have fixed it myself, but I thought I'd look around.'

Harry ... that was his name, he said ... was anxious to show her around his quarters. He was proud of his freezer room, wall ovens, dishwashing machine.

'We run the meals on the hatch system,' he said, 'since although Mr. Bower has run to everything else, he hasn't run to waitresses. It's better, anyway, for folk to see what they're getting.' As he talked, Harry made a large pot of tea and joined her at one of the tables. He put down a plate of raisin scones.

'You think this kitchen's good, you should see the other,' he told Jane.

'The other ... oh, you mean the Baron's? I mean Mr. Bower's?'

'No, Boss mostly eats with us.'

'But there's children.' Perhaps they were his housekeeper's family, Jane thought.

'Yes. Their mother's away for a spell. But he likes them to eat over there. Better for kids, you know.'

Jane did not know, she believed children should eat *en famille*, she believed family men should remain with their family. But before she could continue on the subject, Harry continued on the 'other' kitchen he had mentioned.

'Strictly secret, not the kitchen itself but what they make there, though I can tell you some of the ingredients I sent over.' Harry tabulated them. 'Powdered milk, glucose, rolled oats——'

'You mean for the horses?'

'That's the reason this place functions,' Harry smiled. 'All this' ... he waved his arm around ... 'is just to keep folk happy doing the function. More tea?'

Jane said it had been a large cup, took it to the machine, thanked Harry and went back to her room.

As soon as the girls came in, she would introduce herself—they probably would be younger than she was; most girl strappers started in their teens and were married before they became seniors. She had been a little older than that herself when she had thought in such a way and maturity should have assured such a conclusion, but ... a shrug ... it hadn't come out as she had dreamed.

She went to the window again; the small clothes were off the line now. She was about to leave to place round some of her things when she glimpsed a figure rotating madly from the wire of the clothes-line, the idle wind being helped vigorously by a junior operator whirling it from the ground. Only two small people wearing identical basin crops that she knew of would do that, Jane thought eagerly, it was precisely the outrageous prank that a certain pair would embark on.

She leaned out, called, 'Robert ... Roberta!' but they did not hear her. She saw them leave the line, climb over their enclosing fence to the stud side, then disappear, undoubtedly on more mischief, for they were an incorrigible ... indirigible, they had said on the ship ... pair.

On the ship. He, the Baron, had been on the ship. So *he* was Father William, the voice they had obeyed so promptly. He was the parent of Robert and Roberta, yet she had never thought of placing them together. She doubted, though, if it would make things any easier for her—that man would be a disciplinarian with his staff as well as his children—but she had taken to the imps, and hurrying to the door she ran down the steps to catch up with them, wherever they had gone, enjoy a reunion.

It was on the last step down that Jane heard the shrill scream. She looked around her, trying to trace the source of the scream—a child's scream, and not, Jane judged, even keeping in mind the naughty traits of the impish duo a cry-wolf scream. Whichever of the twins had cried out had really meant the alarm. Meant it urgently.

'Robert, Roberta!' she called, hoping that the scream would come again, since not yet knowing the layout of the place she had no idea which way to turn. Though surely, she thought frantically, someone else in this vast settlement, this—well, this small town you could almost say, had heard. She looked back to the quarters. No one in sight. Perhaps Harry in the kitchen ... But there was no time to check. She remembered from Little Down how completely far away a person can be at even a hundred yards. Once one of the fillies had fallen and—— But not to waste time on thoughts now, she had to find the source of that one urgent cry, and at once.

Jane ran forward, looking left and right as she hurried, hoping desperately for someone, anyone. A strapper returning, a hand sweeping out a stable, a gardener, a handy man, anyone who could direct her to the possible source of a child's scream. Help her.

There was no one at all.

'Robert ... Roberta!' she shouted again. Surely they would reply, even if it was another scream. She listened for the scream, she waited for it. Prayed for it.

Now she was running between what seemed unending small buildings, machine rooms, fodder rooms, all the usual offices associated with a stud. Then there was a row of neat bungalows, the married quarters probably, she thought vaguely, surely someone, a wife, a resting hand, should be around.

No one.

Jane could not have said afterwards how long she would have run, to the end of the plateau, perhaps, even to a cliff edge to peer desperately (and stupidly, since the cry could not have penetrated from that far) over, had she not glimpsed, between the tight buildings, a sparkling patch of blue.

She ran some yards before the fact of that blue hit her. Blue! In a world of unrolling green! Blue in that circumstance must mean water, pool water. There was a pool, and the children had gone to it. That scream had been when one of them had fallen in. But there had been no scream after it. Could it mean that the other one had gone to help, and had——

She did not know how well the children swam, for that matter she did not know whether they swam at all. They had looked jealously down on the Tourist pool on the *Southern Princess*, but that had been because there had been fun going on, not because they envied the swimming it offered them, for had they wanted to swim they could have done it in their own quite superior First-Class pool.

Jane had retraced her steps to the patch between the buildings where she had glimpsed the blue now. It was still there, so it hadn't been a trick of her imagination, she had not been seeing the sky in reverse, and, turning her direction, she raced towards the shining rectangle, wondering fearfully why she could glimpse no sign of life there.

Then as she got nearer she saw that it was not the usual pool, but a pool that had been built exclusively for horses. For a moment Jane knew a fierce anger that the man could have seen to a pool for his horses before he had seen to his children. And *he* had said of her 'pony high priestess!' She saw that the reason nothing or nobody had been in sight was that the pool, because of its purpose, was much deeper than usual, that its walls were twice the rise, that the eventual capacity of the pool twice the expected amount, but that just now it was only semi-filled.

Because of this, the walls, the depth, the water amount, all making for concealment, Jane had to run right up to the

42

edge before she could check.

Yes, there they were. One face downward, the other trying to manipulate Roberta ... or was it Roberta trying to manipulate Robert? ... to an upward position again. The first twin must have entered from the shallow end, the ramp end, but like pools for people, horse pools evidently deepened as well, what was worse unmistakably deepened much more abruptly. Even though the pool was not yet filled, at the end where they struggled it was far too deep for a child.

It was too deep for these two. Even as Jane sized up the position, Roberta ... or Robert ... lost grasp of the other child, then went under as well.

CHAPTER THREE

AFTERWARDS Jane could not remember jumping in, she could not have said whether she ran to the ramp and waded out, or whether she leapt directly into the deeper end from the other side of the pool. All she remembered being aware of in retrospect was the sudden contact of water, then the feel of Robert's basin crop ... for it was Robert face downward and Roberta who had screamed ... as she turned the boy over. She did not remember pushing Roberta to the shallows, and, still holding tightly on to Robert, giving the girl a hearty breath-encouraging slap between her shoulders.

Then she had turned to the boy twin. She had wasted no time. Perhaps he had been under only briefly ... that, anyway, was her desperate hope ... perhaps Roberta's scream had resounded not on her brother's contact with the water but on his subsequent turning over into the water, but she still wasn't taking any chances. Bending across the child, she had begun breathing evenly into his mouth.

Vaguely she had heard Roberta sobbing beside her ... thank heaven it had been the girl on the pool side and not in the water, for though boys act quicker, are more resourceful, a female screams, and without that alerting and summoning scream——

She had heard, still vaguely, Roberta's sobs turning to sniffly noises of apparent relief, heard her say: 'Father William, it's R-Robert.'

She had felt herself pushed aside, then, still knee-deep in the pool, she had watched William Bower cover Robert's entire face, not just his mouth but nose too, with his own large one. She had heard his deep breaths.

Within a minute, Robert said: 'Am I alive?'

'You don't deserve to be.'

44

'Why are you giving me the kiss of life?'

'There's many more things I'd sooner give you, young man!'

'Really——' Jane could not stand it any longer; this was no way to talk to a child who had just cheated death.

William Bower read the reason for her indignation. 'He was a long way off snuffing it,' he announced brutally. 'In fact he could have recovered quite nicely under your own much gentler administering.'

'I could, too,' regretted Robert, 'only I felt too tired, so I just stopped there. If I'd known you were taking over, Father William, I would have got better, though. Jane doesn't have bristly hairs on her lips like you.'

'I should hope not, it's not a female ambition. Can you get up now?'

'Yes.' Robert rose a little unsteadily, but he made it to the edge. 'I was leaning over and I fell in.' He must have decided an explanation was called for.

A quick look at William Bower's face told Jane that this was not enough, and, though he had the sense not to question the boy in his soaked state, he did slip in a warning.

'Run back now and get Teresa to put you into a hot bath.' A pause. 'I'll have more to say later.'

'Was that necessary?' Jane asked as the twins ran off.

'The hot bath?'

'You know what I mean.'

'You mean the reckoning. Yes, it is necessary.'

'But you could have waited till the shock wore off.'

'Never wait, drive the lesson home as soon as the thing happens. Shall I do that now with you?' He had narrowed his eyes on her.

'I have no lesson coming,' she retorted.

He considered this. 'No, you acted pretty slickly, Miss Sidney. My thanks for your resourcefulness.'

'Can I have any post-mortems afterwards,' she inserted shortly, 'the same as Robert? I'm wet and uncomfortable.'

'Run in at once. Soak. Shoot out your clothes to be

45

laundered. Then——'

'Then?'

'Come to my office for a recuperative brandy.'

'Tea will do.'

'Have what you like,' he shrugged. 'I'll be having brandy.'

'But still in the office?'

'I said so.'

'Where,' she asked, 'is the office?'

'In my house.'

'Where the children are?'

'Yes. Unfortunately.'

'Un——' Jane did not finish, she felt too disgusted.

She went back to her quarters, grateful that everyone still seemed out and that she did not have to explain her bedraggled appearance. She did not soak, but she did shower vigorously. When eventually she emerged, dressed, then crossed over to the house within the enclosure, she was rosy and scrubbed, her short hair had curls with damp-hanging ends.

Teresa ... she supposed it was Teresa ... was a smiling Italian, and she showed Jane into the office. A tray of tea awaited, but, as he had said, he was taking brandy.

'I have my meals at the motel, or big house,' he tossed. 'You could say this is my wet canteen.'

'Yes, Harry told me you ate over there. He said' ... the slightest of pauses ... 'the twins eat here.'

'Of course. Adult talk, particularly stud and stable talk, is not always for tender ears. Tender, did I say? That pair?' He gave a dry laugh.

She would have liked to have given him her opinion of family, but he did not wear a receptive expression and he did not follow up the subject.

'Will your clothes be all right after their dunking?' he asked. 'Any you have a doubt about report to the bookkeeper. He'll see to a recompense.'

'Thank you.'

'No, thank you for saving ... or at least making the gesture, for, thank heaven, it wasn't needed ... the kids' lives. Why the little devils went there is beyond me.'

'I would say it was a natural consequence. It's a warm dry day.'

'So you would forgive two brats going out of bounds to try themselves in a horse pool?'

'If they have no pool of their own, yes.'

'And why should I build a pool for them?'

'Why should you ...' she echoed aghast. Pony high priestess, indeed! This man put everything, even his chilren, second to horses. Though *his* reason, she added to add more fuel to her disgust, would be entirely monetary.

'I won't argue about that,' she said coldly.

'I had no intention of arguing,' he said more coldly back. Before she could make any rejoinder, he asked: 'Tea all right?'

'Thank you.'

He had lit his pipe and now the smoke wreaths were weaving upward.

'So you knew the children on the ship?'

'Yes, I met them. We became friendly.'

'Good God!' he disbelieved.

Angry, she retorted, 'I suppose that does seem unlikely to you.'

'Unlikely is the understatement of the year!'

A few minutes went past.

'How was it you came to rescue Robert?'

'I saw the children crossing from the house, recognized them, then went off after them. It was on the bottom step that I heard the scream.' She gave a remembering shiver. 'I'm glad it was Robert who fell in, if it had been Roberta he would have jumped first without screaming as she did. It's the girls who scream.' She became aware that he was looking at her with that one raised eyebrow, and she squirmed.

'So you raced to lend succour?'

47

'Not exactly, I didn't know where to go. No one was around to ask. But luckily I saw a glimpse of the pool between some buildings.'

'Yes. I think it's a good idea, don't you?' He said it quite seriously, she saw in anger. 'A race across a beach, then a plunge through breakers would be preferable for a horse,' he went on, oblivious of her reception, 'but failing that——' He attended his pipe, and she watched him mutinously.

He did not even notice. That was the maddening part. He unmistakably believed he was doing the right thing supplying his horses with a pool while his children, while they——

'So you haven't seen around the place yet?' he broke in.

'No.'

'Then finish your tea.' He made it sound like an invitation, but she heard an order there. However, she wanted to examine her place of employment at some time, so it might as well be now, and under the boss's guidance; at least a boss should know all the answers.

'I have finished.' She got up. As they reached the door she asked: 'How are the children?'

'In bed. Strangely enough they submitted without protest. Must have been tuckered out.'

Jane thought to herself, remembering the way they had obeyed his voice on the ship, that it had been him and not the weariness that had had the effect. She followed him out of the house and through the gate to the stud.

'First, the kitchen,' William Bower said, 'and what goes with it. Not the human roast beef variety ... possibly you've seen that already.'

'Only it was tea and scones,' she nodded.

'Here' ... they had reached a building, neat, immaculate like all the buildings ... 'the magic formulas are dreamed up.'

'Are they magic?'

He grinned. 'Nothing is really magic with horseflesh, but

you can have a jolly good try by adopting good diet additives.' He led her in, and she stood in disbelief at benches of chrome and tile.

'Why not?' He said it defensively, and she knew she should have anticipated that and not shown her surprise. This man was before all else a businessman. His business was horses, these concoctions being encased in pellets were to make the business bigger and better. All the same, such equipment...

To divert his attention from the feelings she felt must show, she asked, 'What's in the formula?'

'Apart from glucose, iron, calcium, which probably you've guessed anyway, it's strictly secret.'

'What about my consignment when they arrive?'

'Your fifth of them,' he corrected.

'They're not to participate?'

'Of course they can participate, but it still doesn't give you the right to learn a formula. For all I know you could be a spy in the camp. Besides——'

'Besides?' she asked furiously.

His answer disarmed her. Anything else he might have said could not have spread oil like these words did.

'I don't know what you delved in at Surrey, Miss Sidney,' he replied sincerely, 'but certainly your fellows don't look in need of formulas.'

'We dealt in soft rain and soft air,' she nodded, suddenly almost unbelievably nostalgic. She had to turn away. To her surprise, for she had not expected understanding ... an understanding of this variety ... from a hard, tough horseman, he went, presumably to examine something, to the other end of the room. When he returned she had herself in control once more.

'I have my own resident nutritionist and pathologist,' he announced.

'Vet?' She was sorry the moment she asked that, it brought up the subject of Rodden Gair, but what she had been inquiring was whether the vet, too, was resident, or only in attendance.

'Everyone resident,' William Bower said, and made no other comment on the matter. He turned to the door again. 'Each stable,' he informed her as they walked out, 'has its own farrier's shop, its own automatic feed-mixing hopper. My silo holds some four thousand bushels of oats.'

'*Could* there be anything else?' she disbelieved as she walked on beside him; she frankly believed no stud could provide more.

'Hot and cold showers for the boys and girls.' He must have remembered what she had said on that last occasion when he had spoken of his stock as that, for he broke off quite abruptly. 'Covered walks,' he went on presently, 'that lead to the sand rolls.'

'I can't understand it,' Jane murmured.

'Can't understand indulging a horse?'

That was not what she had meant, she had been thinking of Rodden's scorn when she had elected to stay back at Little Down to see Melinda through her foaling, yet Rodden Gair, she thought, had come from this stud. It seemed odd that in spite of all the luxury, all the indulgences, this man's employee had raised his brows at a simple human kindness. It made it all the more positive to Jane that any balm given to any of the stock here at Bowers welled from one reason only: Money.

He was talking, so reluctantly she had to listen.

'It has to be like this.' He was excusing the indulgences. 'Australia is not a "natural" for horseflesh as are England, Ireland, America ... you can include New Zealand. We have to fight for what we achieve. Those others get it on a gold plate. Here's the clinic.'

'Vet variety, of course.'

'I naturally run a casualty for the staff, but then there's always transport available to fly them over to Fetherfell across the Divide, which runs a fine hospital, and in which I support a ward.'

'Of course.' Jane could not help that.

50

'We have a girl in here now ... I mean we have a filly,' he corrected himself quickly. 'Bessie has leg trouble.'

He went up to the pretty, chunky grey and Jane went, too, and fondled the satin head.

'However, we still follow the old rule of operating in an open paddock,' William Bower related. He laughed ruefully. 'You can put out thousands on a hospital, some more again on an X-ray machine, a sterilizing plant, but when it comes to a crisis...' He shrugged.

'It's usually like that.' In spite of herself, of her determination to stand aloof, Jane said it eagerly. Experiences came pouring out ... she and Rusty spending days in a row in the rough acre on Stately Lady, because, in spite of her name, that elegant chestnut had refused to foal anywhere else.

'Yes,' William Bower broke in just as eagerly, 'that's the way it goes. Sometimes I think that love is not cloud nine, as the song goes, but ten cold nights in a paddock.'

Love is ten cold nights in a paddock. It had been eleven, Jane remembered, because Stately Lady had been lazy, and the paddock had been a meadow, but——

Jane was unaware that she was looking up at the man, unaware that he was looking back at her.

Then ... abruptly ... she became aware. She looked away again.

'You've just about seen it all.' His voice came matter-of-factly, she could not have believed it was the same man who had broken in before: 'Sometimes I think that love is not cloud nine but ten cold nights in a paddock.'

He asked: 'Shall we go back? It's the only place actually to go, unless you drive out and go over a cliff.'

'But there must be roads to the valley.'

'Glorified tracks only.'

'But the timber down there has to get out.'

'Of course, but not by way of Plateau. No, the timbermen, hop-men, eucalyptus oil men ... yes, they go in for a mixed plate in the valley ... avail themselves of the road to

51

the coast. You could say we're fairly isolated up here, we're the top of the tree, so to speak, no way to get out except to fly or climb down, and that's why we have to be self-sufficient.'

They had reached the centre point of the stud again, it almost could have been called a village square, Jane thought, for Bowers was large enough to be a small village.

'So you swim,' he broke in casually.

'Yes,' Jane said, a little surprised.

'And the kids don't.'

Now she was considerably surprised, surprised at a father not knowing that. However, she did not know really about the children herself. She had not found out on the ship, and she had not really found out here, either. All she had known when she had reached the horse pool's edge was that a child was in difficulties and that the other child had made it difficult for herself by trying to help.

'It could be,' she said, 'that Robert stunned himself in the fall.'

'I didn't see any evidence on him. I'll question him later, and if he and Roberta can't swim, then——' He was interrupted in what he was going to say by the bookkeeper coming over to discuss some matter. Jane was introduced to Stan Littleton, invited to call in to see how his side of the stud business functioned, then, as the men went off together, she turned back to the digs.

She had yet to meet the nutritionist, pathologist, probably a dozen grooms, a dozen exercising hands, and—the vet. She did not dwell on that.

A cantering behind her attracted her attention, and she turned to see two female strappers coming in from their duties. They could have been girls from Little Down had any girls beside herself served at Little Down, they could have been stablehands anywhere, with their fresh faces, bright eyes and wind-combed hair. They were young. Well, she had expected that. Only the unlucky in love reached her own age, Jane thought, without that confirming ring.

At that thought her eyes had dropped instinctively to the girl, Maureen...

Jane would have recognized that ring in any corner of the world. She expected there could be many aquamarines with silver filigree settings, but there is always something about your own ring...

Your own ring. What was she thinking about? She had sent the ring back to Rodden, it had not belonged to her any more.

And now, unless she was mistaken, Maureen wore it. Well, that made sense. Maureen was a very pretty girl, and Rodden, besides liking pretty girls, had worked here.

Jane accepted the girls' invitation to join them in a cup. She walked behind them to the canteen, answering their questions, asking questions of her own. But never the question she wanted to ask. It wasn't that there was any hurt left, she had accepted everything long ago, it was just that she wanted to *know*, for if you knew, then naturally you handled things better, and if Maureen was engaged to Rodden, even though he now worked away from here there could come a time when she, Jane, and Rodden met up again. So it must be well-handled, Jane thought.

She was trying to handle her cup without spilling any tea, and it was difficult because at the same time she was endeavouring to manipulate herself into a better ring-observing position ... *just to be sure* ... when the canteen telephone pealed.

Harry answered it and said, 'Yes, Boss.' He turned to the tables and called: 'Mr. Bower wants to see you, Miss Sidney.'

Jane did not move. The house was no further than an enclosed yard away, surely, even though he was the boss——

Harry finished: 'Over there.'

The topic of the Boss's call appeared concluded. The girls looked at her expectantly, then went on to something else. Everyone in the room looked quietly expectant ...

expectant of her immediate obedience. What an autocrat this fellow was! Again ... many times again ... Jane thought that.

But to sit on, to wait for him to come to her, and somewhere within her Jane accepted the fact that he wouldn't come, would only draw attention, something she did not want. Finishing her tea—at any rate she did that—Jane got up, nodded around, and left.

William Bower opened the door for her. Jane could hear dishes being clattered and presumed that Teresa was busy with nursery tea.

'I've found out that the brats can't swim,' he said, leading the way to the room where she had spoken with him earlier today. 'I examined Robert for any knock-out marks. No, he simply overbalanced, fell in, then couldn't right himself. A fine state of affairs.'

Fine, indeed! rankled Jane.

'So I asked him. He hated telling—went around it all ways before it came out.'

'That's natural,' Jane defended.

'Not being able to swim isn't. I intend to right it at once.'

'Where? The horse pool?'

'No.'

'There's another?'

'No, but there will be. I intend building one for the staff.'

For the staff! And yet when it came to his two children——

'However,' William Bower went on, 'that will take time ... months. Besides, even if it was fenced, grown-ups could still suffer from young trespassers, and no adult wants a youngster monkeying around.'

'So what do you do?'

'Down the valley we have the Urara River. There's a section of it that all of us residents have made safe and attractive. Thousands of tons of sand have been put down, old

54

logs removed. The shelf is very gradual. In fact you could say it's a real charmed stretch.'

'The children will learn there?'

He was lighting his pipe.

'That depends on you.'

'On me?'

'Depends on whether you'll teach them.'

'I'd love to teach them. I feel very strongly about children swimming. But I came here to work, remember, not to——'

'You have different ideas of work, then, than I have. To teach that pair an Australian crawl——'

'I believe dog-paddle will do as a start—after all, the purpose is to bring them to a pitch of saving their own lives, not winning a race.'

'Then will you?'

'My consignment——' she began.

'Won't be out for over a week.'

She looked at him levelly. 'If you're really saying I have nothing to do with Bowers, only to do with what Rusty is consigning to Bowers, say it.'

'One-fifth of it,' he put in.

'Are you saying that?'

'No. I'm asking you to teach the kids to swim. The same salary as if you were working on the horses.'

As she sat silent, he probed, 'What gives, Miss Sidney? I'm making a straightforward request of you. Does everything I say have to be met with suspicion?'

'I wasn't suspecting, I was disbelieving.'

'Isn't it the same?'

'Not that. I was disbelieving that a parent couldn't see to such a basic thing for a child as swimming.'

'Yes,' he agreed coolly. 'But then they're exceptional parents.'

She looked at him in more disbelief, disbelieving now that a man could not only hold such an opinion of himself, but openly flaunt it.

'I'm not asking for any excuses' ... *he* wouldn't, Jane seethed ... 'but when you have two exceptional people, you can't expect the niceties of ordinary parents.'

'Since when has preservation been a "nicety"?' she flashed.

'Yes, that was the wrong word,' he conceded. 'What I really meant to say was that Gareth has always been pre-occupied with his gift, while my cousin-in-law——'

'Your cousin-in-law?' Jane broke in.

He raised that brow again. 'Isn't there such?' he shrugged.

'You mean—the wife of your cousin?'

'My cousin Gareth's wife Dorothy.' William Bower paused a moment, his eyes raking Jane's face. 'Owners,' he informed her drily, 'of the brats.'

CHAPTER FOUR

Jane sat silent, wishing desperately she could think of something to say, something to divert his amused attention from her flag-red cheeks and her obvious air of guilt. For she *had* been guilty without inquiring first of putting these children down as his, any naughtiness they flaunted as his fault.

But it was no use. Her mother had always laughed over Jane's air of guilt, she had said her daughter was an open book. Now the man opposite was reading the open book and smiling lopsidedly at her discomfiture.

'You thought——' he said, then laughed.

'Why not?' Words came at last, only not the off-putting words Jane had searched for. She had wanted to close the subject, or at least change it, but now she was continuing it instead. 'You had them in your care,' she accused indignantly, 'they called you Father William.'

'My name is William. In case you've forgotten, it's William Bower.'

'I hadn't forgotten. But why Father William?'

'You should have asked them that yourself.'

'I did,' she recalled unwillingly. She recalled, too, the answer. Roberta's answer. ' "William's his name," the girl twin had reported, "and once he said he'd kick Robert down the stairs." ' Jane also recalled, this time from Robert, that a bucket of water had been strategically placed.

So Father William was not their paternal parent but their second cousin. Jane worked out the relationship laboriously.

'Lewis Carroll,' she heard herself murmuring aloud.

'From the sound of him once as beggared by kids as I am,' William Bower inserted.

'I wouldn't say that.'

57

'Miss Sidney, you're not being asked to say anything.'

'Only do something.'

'Yes, teach them to swim ... only we're not finished with Father William yet, are we? Let's get the thing straight.'

'You mean your guardianship of your second cousins?'

'Is that how it goes?' he asked admiringly. 'No, I didn't mean exactly that, I meant your fool conclusion.'

'I don't think it was foolish. You had them with you on the ship.'

'Where evidently you didn't associate the three of us as belonging.'

'And you have them now.' She ignored the interruption. 'Surely anyone would conclude then that you were their parent.'

He was leaning across the desk to her. He did not speak for several moments, and every moment built up a curious nervousness in Jane. She could not have said why, but it was all she could do not to get up and run out of the room. He could be very frightening, this Father William of the children's, no wonder they obeyed him on the double.

'Look at me,' he ordered at last, but Jane looked anywhere but at him, 'look at me, then tell me if that is the sort of arrangement you think *I* would have in my married life.'

'I don't know what arrangement you'd have. I don't even know if you're married.'

'Then I'm not. Also I would have things very differently. My youngsters would be with me, and so, by heaven, would my wife.'

'Why are you telling me this?' she asked.

'Because you have the presumption to associate me with a position like this.'

'Is it that important?'

'You appeared to think so before.'

'I meant,' she corrected herself, 'is it that important that I should be told so forcibly?'

That stopped him a moment. Then he said in a rather surprised voice: 'Yes ... yes, it is.'

He was staring at her. She felt it. It had to be feeling, for she was not looking back at him. She found she could not look.

'What kind of talents have the children's parents?' she tried to divert.

He permitted diversion. He said, 'They paint. Dorothy does portraits, Gareth landscapes. They're both good. And that's not just someone who doesn't know art but knows what he likes talking, critics who do know are agreed that the two Courtneys——'

'Courtneys?' she echoed.

'You've heard of them?'

'Of course. I think most people have.' Dorothy Courtney with her exquisite child studies, Gareth Courtney with his vigorous canvases had reached the European scene as well as the scene in Australia.

'Then I'm to look for talent in the children?' Jane said with enthusiasm.

'No.' She glanced inquiringly at him. 'Not essentially. They're adopted children. You might remember I said the owners, not the parents, of the brats. There were none forthcoming of their own, so they adopted this pair. Gareth, my father's sister's child, and his wife Dorothy felt in their absorbing life that they must give out as well as take in.'

'That was good of them.'

'As well as gifted, they're good people. This branch of the family' ... he made a gesture to himself ... 'must rely on the goodness, I'm afraid, for I have no talent.'

'The stud?' she asked in all seriousness, for to her way of thinking a stud was much more than the usual occupation.

'Only requires a pair of strong hands.'

She did not comment. She was thinking suddenly and sharply of his 'love is ten cold nights in a paddock', and the quiet manner in which it had touched her.

'It must be hard for the children having their father and mother away,' Jane said a little breathlessly, afraid she might voice those other thoughts.

'It's the first time it's happened, though Gareth and Dorothy sometimes go solo. I suppose,' he had the grace to submit, 'I should keep their talents in mind when I say it wouldn't happen to me.'

So he was on to that again, that masterful head-of-the-family act.

'But then,' he went on, 'I would never choose an artist.'

'No,' she agreed, incensed, 'you would consider all things beforehand—as in a stud.'

'Of course. Surely, as a strapper, as someone among horseflesh, you're not examining me on that? You must have learned from my uncle the necessity of acquiring desired qualities in a brood mare, the opposite desired qualities in the sire. For instance, a long-backed mare should be crossed with a heavy-ribbed stallion, and——'

'I was speaking,' Jane broke in, 'of you, not your business.'

'Then I, too,' he said coolly, 'would know what would be advisable for me to take on, what wouldn't be.'

'Don't you mean whom?' Jane corrected.

'I told you I was without talent,' he came back, 'as well as being unartistic, my grammar shows holes. I'm no man of words.'

Yet—love is ten cold nights in a paddock, Jane thought.

'No,' William Bower went on, 'my type would need a more basic mate than an artist.'

'A dairymaid, perhaps,' Jane said flippantly.

'Admirable. A country girl would be a very advisable choice. Only' . . . a pause . . . 'never a stud variety.'

She had not been looking at him, intentionally not looking at him. But now . . . angrily . . . she did. He stared intentionally back at her, and for some reason she thought of old Rusty and his 'mutual look'. This look was the very opposite to that. She waited.

'Rodden Gair,' William Bower reminded her in a low voice.

'What about him?'

'You tossed him, didn't you?'

'No, I——'

'Oh, we all know you put it in fancy words, but you showed Rodden where to go.'

'Is that what he said?'

'He didn't say anything. He just came back, and a month later a ring came back. I expect he should be grateful at least for that.'

'You've only half the truth. I was coming, but Melinda——'

'You threw him over,' he said factually.

'All right, if you want it like that.'

'How did *you* want it?' he came in. 'As dedication? As work first? "I want to come," the pony high priestess intones, "but——" ' William Bower laughed scornfully. 'So,' he concluded, 'no female strapper for me.'

'And yet you're devoted to your work,' she baited.

He reddened slightly. 'It's just that to me. Just work.'

'But work close to your heart,' she suggested. 'The "girls" and the "boys".' She quoted him, not caring if he reddened properly now from the embarrassment he had shown before. He was a very male male, she thought. ' "Love is ten cold nights in a paddock," ' she added triumphantly.

'Trust a female to store that up!' he came in acidly.

'I didn't store it, the words struck a chord in me, because once I'd spent ten plus one. Her name was Stately Lady.'

'Not Melinda?' he said like a whiplash.

'You store up things, too, don't you, Mr. Bower.'

There was a pause, a long one.

Then: 'In a stud, the nearest to you is the vet,' William Bower said quietly. 'Rodden was my vet. When he returned from England he was a broken man.' He tapped at his pipe.

Jane looked at him helplessly. There were many things she could have said, but she could see he had closed himself up; you cannot explain to a shut door. She wondered what Rodden had told him, but she did not wonder about Rodden's attitude; he always had been a master of attitudes, she knew that now.

'I sent him away,' William Bower announced factually. When she did not question him, he explained, 'Married staff here move into the flats.'

'Yes, I saw them.'

'One was to have been for Rodden and his English wife. I couldn't have him staying on here to pass each day by what might have been his haven.'

The falseness of Rodden infuriated Jane. She took it out on William Bower. She said deliberately, 'When do the violins play?'

'You're a very cold, collected, calculating young woman, Miss Sidney. You stayed behind in Surrey because to leave might have endangered the hand-out you anticipated eventually from my uncle.'

Rodden had been long before that, she had never anticipated anything, Rusty's gift had been a complete surprise, but all at once Jane felt too tired to fight back.

'Yes,' she said recklessly, 'I did just that. I'm sorry about Rodden. Evidently he suffers more in retrospect; he wasn't what I call a broken man when he left me. Also he appears to have recovered. Maureen is wearing my—wearing a similar ring to the one I returned.'

'Rodden is vetting at one of my smaller satellite studs over at Fetherfell, across the Divide. On my advice he took out his flying licence, and I've provided him with a small plane, so he can visit Maureen as any ordinary suburban man can visit his fiancée.'

'Maureen is that, then?'

'She is.'

'That's very nice,' Jane said. 'Now can we return to what you wanted to see me about?'

'The swimming,' he nodded, allowing the closing of the subject. 'Pending the release of your first consignment in several weeks, instead of making ordinary strapping your

62

way of earning your keep, you can keep an eye on the twins.'

'Will the parents agree to that?'

'They'll be very pleased,' he assured her. 'They don't usually both leave home together, but this time Dorothy was asked to do a course in Paris, and Gareth was finishing a client's order in Singapore. I took the kids across to see their father for a break for all of us. Only' ... feelingly ... 'it wasn't. I never considered Paris except as too unsuitable for nippers like them. But' ... feelingly again ... 'Paris couldn't have been worse for me.'

'Nor for them. They were bored up in First.'

'There were fewer people to drive mad in First,' he said back. 'School had been arranged, but it fell through, or at least the school the parents wanted. So there was nothing for it than to be inflicted. If you can ease that infliction for several weeks ...'

'You dislike children, don't you?' She looked at him pityingly.

'As a matter of fact in my unguarded moments I like them.'

'Why must moments be guarded?'

'Because of people like you,' he said at once, 'people ready to pounce, ready to remember and relate back.'

'Boys and girls,' she recited slyly, 'ten cold nights in a paddock. I promise you I'll remember just as well when you're unguarded over Robert and Roberta.'

'Only them?' he asked unexpectedly.

She looked at him in surprise, but whatever had impelled him to speak like that had left him. He looked back, and except that there were steps on the verandah outside the look would have gone on, that odd uncalculated look ...

Someone knocked, and, at William Bower's call, came in.

'Miss Sidney, this is my present Bowers vet. Tim Harris. Tim, Jane Sidney.'

Jane turned to a stocky but well-proportioned young man

eyeing her with unconcealed approval. The hand that took hers was strong and friendly, and she grasped his back in the same manner. He seemed nice, she thought.

'It's Sovereign Gold,' Tim said to his boss, 'that old chronic hoof condition is playing up again.'

William Bower turned to Jane. 'Sovereign Gold has good connections. I had hopes of the colt proving himself as a top-class stayer this year. He's galloped brilliantly on occasions, but failed just as frequently.'

'It sounds rather like it might be pedal-ostitis,' said Jane, remembering an instance at Little Down, and the inflammation of the pedal bone that one of their boys had suffered.

Tim was looking appreciatively at Jane. 'You're so right. As soon as there's pressure on the hoof, Sovereign is in severe pain. We've taken more X-rays. Perhaps you'd like to see them, Miss Sidney, see Sovereign.'

'Oh, I would!' Jane stood up.

She followed the vet to the door, rather relieved to be finished with Bower, but before she reached the verandah William Bower's voice stopped her.

'You left this, Miss Sidney.'

'Excuse me,' Jane returned.

The man was standing at the table. He did not offer anything, and she realized he only had called her back to say something.

'He's even more vulnerable than Gair,' he said coolly.

She followed his trend, and flushed with indignation, but before she could speak, Bower went on.

'I wouldn't want Tim hurt, too. And you do rather gather vet scalps, don't you?' An unsmiling smile.

'Yes, Mr. Bower,' she said, 'they're my favourite scalps.'

'No boss's scalps?'

'I've only had one boss, and he was elderly.'

'You must try a younger variety.'

'And be scalped myself?'

'Miss Sidney, you read my thoughts.' He nodded carlessly as she turned to join Tim again.

But he did come to the door to call out to his vet.

'The lady has had a long day, Tim, a rather eventful day. Don't keep her too long.' As with everything that Willam Bower said, it sounded a suggestion but was really an order. Tim did not seem to mind being ordered, however. He promised to look after Jane, and they went off.

Sovereign Gold was in the paddock where the trouble had taken him. Jane examined the pedal bone and confided a few things that Rusty had done to Silver Bell. Rusty had been no vet, but he had had a lot of experience ... and a lot of success. Tim listened attentively, and Jane recalled how Rodden had smiled thinly and patronizingly over the old man's wisdoms. Tim was entirely different. She liked him, too, liked his friendly approach, liked his manliness. But ... stepping back a pace, and Tim looking up questioningly, and a little disappointed ... she must watch her step with William Bower's eyes on her.

'I'm sorry, Tim, but it's been a long day.' It had been a very long day, she could hardly credit it was only one day. But then they had berthed in the early a.m., and flying made minutes of miles.

At once Tim was apologizing, taking her over to her digs.

Jane went up the stairs at once, deciding to skip dinner, even though she wanted to meet the rest of the stud. She passed Maureen in the corridor, and the girl flashed her a bright smile. She can't know, Jane thought. I hope she doesn't know in the future. There's always a tension, a distrust in a situation like this. The thing to do is not to meet Rodden because Rodden is the only way Maureen can find out. I don't think William Bower would tell her, he sounded quite fond of Maureen. She seems a very reasonable child, too, but no girl wants another girl's ring.

She showered ... the second time since she had come to Bowers she shrugged under the spray ... came out, got into a gown and made a cup of tea.

She didn't finish it, though, she was too weary. She

hoped she was not too over-tired to sleep. At first sleep did elude her, and then she was drifting. She was saying: 'Love is ten cold nights in a paddock,' then changing it to eleven in a meadow.

An English meadow. With Rusty. Not an Australian paddock with cold, efficient, estimating, enigmatic William Bower.

'Father William,' she mumbled. And slipped off.

It was bright daylight when she opened her eyes. She wondered drowsily what had aroused her at this particular moment, she felt there had been a little noise somewhere. Something attracted her attention at the window, and she saw it was a sheet of paper with badly printed letters: HURRY UP.

She smiled, but wiped the smile off as she crossed to the window and saw the twins on the roof top above her dangling down the sign. Luckily, she thought, feeling with William on this occasion, the roof was a flat type.

'Hurry up!' They repeated their printed message.

'You shouldn't be there!' she shouted.

'We wouldn't if you were up.'

'You're taking us down the valley,' said Roberta.

'Father William says so,' called Robert.

'You're bad children, you could be killed!' she scolded.

'Everyone can be killed. The window could drop down on your head.'

'Robert could drop on it,' Roberta said admiringly, admiring her brother's greater daring in leaning over.

Quickly Jane stepped back, and at the same time saw the note. That was what must have awakened her, the sound of the note being pushed under the door. She took it up.

'Dear Miss Sidney, Apropos our discussion [apropos! So he was not entirely adverse to words!] in the garages you'll find a small car for your use. Ask Donnelly. I have no doubt that a stablehand can drive a car as well as ride a horse. If not, we must think of something else. Please be careful, I have every wish to return both minors in a sound state. Careful for yourself as well, though I doubt if I need remind you of this, as you would know, as I do, that a forfeited fifth share would only benefit me, which should be sufficient incentive for you not to take risks. There's only one track, so you can't lose the way. Harry will pack a hamper. Don't forget towels. Have a bearable day.

W. Bower.'

She put the letter down, dressed as quickly as she could between crossing to the window to see if the twins were still intact, then she ran down the stairs to the canteen, collected a hamper that William Bower must have ordered, and emerged to find the children waiting for her.

'We thought you'd never come. Did you bring your swimming togs?'

'Yes. Did you?'

Their skips and whoops proclaimed that they had. The three of them crossed to the garages.

Donnelly, also prepared, had a manoeuvrable small car awaiting them. Jane found the gears familiar, and within minutes the trio were on a track that Donnelly indicated.

It ran, a narrow earth ribbon, through the lush green swathe of the plateau until the rolling paddocks ended, then it descended cautiously, for caution was needed down the steep cliffside, past peaks, gorges, sudden deep gulches, great isolated rocks, splaying waterfalls into a valley. Between keeping her attention strictly on the track, Jane darted brief looks ahead, and saw, in the distance, that paddocks fanned out once again from the valley towards the coast, mostly cleared paddocks for cultivation, but in the dent of every small rise in them blue-smudged shadows from the overlooking mountains in the unfolding golden-green of the grass.

'It's beautiful!' Jane had stopped the car.

'The pool,' came an impatient duet from the back seat. With a little sigh, Jane reduced another gear and started carefully down once more.

She would have loved to have known the trees. When she asked the twins they said, 'Gums, of course.'

'Not all of them. Some of these are quite different.'

'Red gum, silver gum, scribbley. There's billions,' they tossed. They were obviously anxious to get to their goal.

There was no trouble in finding the pool. Rounding a bend at the bottom of the cliff, a grassy bank under willows with a wide golden sand frontage ... the gift of the Urara residents, Jane remembered from William Bower ... greeted them.

It was a charming spot; the residents could not have chosen better. The water idled by in a gentle pace that would never alarm new swimmers, but it moved sufficiently to keep it clear and singing, in fact the only addition to its shine and sparkle was a floating leaf.

Also, a man, swimming now towards Jane, lifting his hand in delighted greeting.

It was John, and, just as delighted, Jane raised her arm and waved back.

'Who is he?' asked Roberta, but she did not wait for an answer. Robert had beaten her in, so there was no time for Jane's explanation.

Jane herself wasted no time as well. William Bower had said that the shelf of the rivulet was a safe and gradual one, but the sparkle of the water was enticing, the children obviously unafraid, so she must be extra careful. She was grateful to John that he caught the purpose and did not hinder her with any talk until the first lesson was over, and the children, a little tired, were launching bark boats from the bank.

They had done exceptionally well, they were fluid children, agile, fit. They would be naturals, Jane thought.

'Perhaps,' said Robert, 'our real mother and father were Olympic swimmers and we've taken after them.' So the twins had been told the truth, Jane gleaned, and evidently, by their contented faces, told in a wise way.

'We were chosen, you know, Jane,' Roberta added casually.

That had been after they had emerged on Jane's insistence almost waterlogged from the stream. Now they lazily launched boats and Jane could turn and greet John.

'I didn't expect you.'

'I told you I was a Uraran.'

'Yes, but it was only yesterday we left the ship.' It seemed impossible to Jane it was only that, so much seemed to have happened.

'You thought it would take me longer,' he nodded. 'I didn't waste any time. Also, I'm just arriving now.'

'You haven't been home, then?'

'No. I always carry trunks for the times when I pass this spot—it's a lovely place, isn't it?'

'It's beautiful.' She told him William Bower's plans for the teaching of the children.

'That's wonderful. I'll be seeing you, then.'

'How far away are you?' she asked.

'You passed it,' he told her.

'I'm sure we didn't pass a house.'

'Like to bet on it?' he grinned. 'Call the kids and we'll go there for lunch'

'I have a hamper.'

'Then you can eat from it if you want to be independent. However' ... the twins, having finished their launching, returning ... 'I make rare Johnny cakes.'

'Johnny cakes!' They took it up in a delighted chorus.

'Why not?' John laughed. 'My name is John.' He turned to Jane. 'I'll take one, you take the other. Follow me.'

Jane hesitated, at once the thought of William Bower crossing her mind, but the first lesson had been successfully concluded, the children were eager to go and ... With a smile she took Robert and got into the small car.

They retraced only a few hundred yards, then turned into

a side track making its own canyon as it wound through thick trees. From his several yards ahead of her, John called of the trees: 'Blackwoods. Sassafras. Mahogany.'

'*Not* all gums,' Jane told Robert.

There were small musk trees and tree ferns, too, fallen logs from dead trees covered with lichen, mosses and old man's beard. In fact there was so much overgrowth and undergrowth that there seemed no room for anything but leaves.

But there was room for a house, Jane found, negotiating a bend after John had, a low, oiled-timber one, looking as at home as though, like the trees encircling it, it had grown there, too.

Delighted, Jane got out. It was a lovely place, built to fit in with the woods, with John's hopfields further along the valley, with the eucalyptus distillery he was telling her he also had, though it was tucked away in a fold of the hill, he said, behind the house. 'I have to include all the variations I can, Jane, these times competition is tough.'

He was making the Johnny cakes, for the twins would give him no peace, he said ruefully, until he produced the promised batch.

'Me, too,' smiled Jane, looking at John's frothing mixture. 'Why,' she asked, 'such a big house?'

'I've always intended it for a family house.' John looked up from his mixing at Jane.

'I hope you have your family, John,' she said.

The Johnny cakes were wonderful, there was not a crumb left. There was also no room in the twins for Harry's offerings. Jane wondered if Harry might tell William Bower about that.

After the meal, John took them down to his timber section, and Jane stood sadly with him by some of the bigger trees marked for cutting.

'Yes, I feel the same,' John nodded, sensing her mood, 'but that's life, Jane. Come and see a brighter side ... at least it goes to provide a brighter life.'

'The hops?'

'Yes.'

It was not a large hop garden, just more bread and butter, John told her, on his plate. Some of the fellows in the district had gone in entirely for hops, he said, and when the picking was on, the valley was worth visiting. New Australians came in as well as the old ones, and the variations in the cooking, and, at night, in the dancing, was exciting.

'We'll come,' promised the twins.

'To pick, too?' asked John. 'Being a small grower I don't hire hands as the others have to do, and I'd be glad of help.' He showed the children and Jane how he had provided vast networks of strung wires for the hops, supported by a forest of poles. 'Self-grown poles,' he boasted.

'Now come and examine the third home-grown product, the distillery. Tell me if you see a difference in the trees, Jane.'

They were certainly gums again, but instead of Robert's 'billions' of varieties, there seemed only one type.

'It happens,' John said when she told him this. 'Sometimes a valley of blue gum builds up a stronghold and won't let anything else in. It doesn't happen frequently, and that's where I'm lucky.'

'Why, John? Don't you like the other gums?' This valley of John's was all blue gum.

'An identical valley of trees makes for a good eucalyptus yield. I'm getting twenty gallons a week from this little acreage, Jane. You could say the oil is the jam on my bread.'

He told her his simple but effective method of piping off and condensing. As he spoke he rolled leaves in his hard workman's hands, and sniffed them, and Jane did the same. They smiled across at each other.

The children had come with them, but must have got bored with the technical explanation and sauntered off. When they did not return in the next ten minutes, Jane started to fuss.

'No need for worry,' insisted John comfortingly, 'though it looks a formidable wood they can't go far where we stand now.'

'The Australian bush——' Jane feared.

'Should be treated with respect, I'll give in, but right here it's a corner, and they can't get out unless they climb out, and I hardly think' ... looking up at the ramparts ... 'they'll do that. I'll give them a cooee ... that means come here, did you know? ... and they'll be bounding back.'

But they didn't bound back. At the end of another five minutes John repeated his assurance of safety, to which Jane replied: 'Perhaps, but I hardly like returning the twins late on my first day.'

He agreed with her on that, and gave another summons, louder than before, following it with: 'Come out, you two, or no more Johnny cakes!'

They came bounding down a track, full of apologies.

'The man in the bush kept us,' panted Roberta.

'Kept you, you mean,' corrected Robert. He added, 'He wanted to sculp her.'

'Scalp should be more like it,' John scolded mildly. 'Don't worry, Jane, I know the old fellow. He comes here now and then ... it's an abandoned woodman's humpy round the next valley and free for all ... to live with nature. Quite harmless.'

'Not so old,' said Roberta, but Jane took no notice of her ... then. She was bustling the children to the car.

'We must get up to the plateau at once.'

Although the climb was steep, the little car took it well. The moment they were on the flat, Jane accelerated to home.

She was garaging the car when Donnelly came across.

'No troubles?' he asked.

'No, everything went wonderfully.'

'Wish I could say that about the stud.' Like all the employees, even though Les Donnelly was a mechanical and

72

not a horse man, the horses played a very big part in his life.

'Anything wrong?'

'The old mare Wendy is foaling. She must be all of twenty-one years.'

'That's advanced,' nodded Jane, then, seeing the concern on Donnelly's face, 'But lots of mares do it successfully.'

'Reckon it's the mare and not the newcomer that's concerning the boss. He loves that old girl.'

'I wonder' ... Jane hesitated ... 'I wonder if I could go across. I haven't got a degree or anything like that, but I have had experience.'

'I reckon that would be real fine, miss,' Donnelly said eagerly. 'As I said, we all love Wendy. Hop in the jeep and I'll take you to the western paddock. That's where the old girl is.'

Forgetting the hamper she had not removed yet but had intended to, glad that she had dropped the children at the house, Jane got into the jeep.

The western paddock was a quarter of a mile away. 'Wendy always foaled here,' Donnelly related. He stopped the jeep by the fence, and Jane got out, climbed some bars, then walked quietly to the small group of men gathered round the foaling Wendy.

William Bower glanced up at her as she came, and had she not known that cool man now she would have said that there was a flicker of gratefulness at her approach. As for Tim, the vet, there was no mere flicker, there was a welcoming smile.

The smile was soon wiped away, though.

'Wendy's no good,' Tim said.

The next ten minutes were a bigger nightmare than Jane ever had with Rusty back at Little Down. For there they had never lost a mother, only horses in general, since horses have their life span, too, and must go on. But never, Jane recalled, a mare in foal.

But now they lost Wendy. The foal was born, an im-

73

petuous filly whose robust fight to enter the world, plus Wendy's advanced years, certainly caused Wendy's death.

But although the mare was haemorrhaging, she lived long enough to give the little girl the first vital feed. Most foals, Jane knew, die without that initial suckling of colostrum, which contains the maternal anti-bodies to protect the baby from disease.

Then Wendy died. She was twenty-one, she had the credit of many children, some of them quite famous, she had enjoyed a full life ... but Jane understood when William Bower pushed his hands, not needed any longer, into his coat pocket and turned and walked away.

Impetuously she ran after him. 'Mr. Bower——'

He wheeled round.

'I'm sorry,' she said.

'She was old,' he replied shortly, but she understood it was only a cover-up.

'I'll watch the foal,' she offered.

'Yes, do that.' He got into his car and went back to the stud. Jane went to the wobbly, spindly-legged little girl, gazing around her with astonished eyes. She wiped her, then said: 'Nine ounces of vegetable extract, dried skim milk, calcium, edible oil, dextrose and glucose was our Little Down formula, failing, of course, a foster-mother.'

'Which we don't have,' said Tim.

'Then if I feed her hourly on that?'

'It will be wonderful,' the vet accepted. He covered Wendy and sighed: 'Green pastures, old girl.'

A float was coming out and Jane took the foal with her into the box. Tim came, too.

'Boss is upset,' he said. 'A man has to be when it's a thing like this.'

But when Jane emerged from the stables after making arrangements with Tim which feeding hours would be hers and which his, William Bower was waiting outside the door for her, and the tone of his voice as he asked her to come across to his office was no longer the tone of a distressed man. In fact he seemed in full control of whatever position he . . . and presumably Jane, since he had come for her . . . found themselves. All his sentimentality was gone, he was hard and cool again.

'Tim and I have come to an agreement regarding the night feeding of the foal,' Jane began. 'During the day we thought the other girls——' She stopped at a dismissive movement of his big hands. 'What is it, Mr. Bower?' she asked.

'You recall our talk yesterday?'

'Very well.'

'I asked you to waive your strapping duties for a while, didn't I, and instead concentrate on the kids.'

'Yes, you did. Then' . . . believing she saw what he was after . . . 'you don't want me to take over Wendy's Pride—we called her that pending——'

'I *wanted*' . . . he made a point of the past tense . . . 'you to take over the twins.'

'And you don't want it now?' she asked.

'I don't know. I do know I want an explanation first.'

'Of what?'

'Your late arrival back from the valley. That was one heck of a long day, Miss Sidney.'

'Yes, it was, but I can explain.'

'Explain, too, an unopened hamper? Harry was quite upset about it. Felt he hadn't made it attractive enough. He came and asked me. In case you don't know, just as with an army, a stud marches . . . should I say canters?' . . . an unamused laugh . . . 'on its stomach. In any concern a cook always stands top in importance, even over the boss, and Harry is a very good cook. I wouldn't care to lose him.' He waited. 'Through you.'

'I'll speak to Harry,' she offered.

'Telling him what? That the three of you were on a diet? That you purchased goodies from the shop that isn't there?'

'No,' said Jane honestly, 'that we had Johnny cakes with John.'

75

He looked at her a long incredulous moment. 'Are they the words of a song? Johnny cakes with John?'

'No, of course not,' she answered sharply, feeling somehow caught-out, and she shouldn't, for really there had been nothing. But still she had the stupid sensation that she had inveigled something, that she had deceived.

'Tell me, please.' His voice was dry.

'When we reached the beach, John was swimming there,' she began.

'Prearranged?'

'Certainly not. He was on his way to his house—he says he always stops for a swim.'

'That adds up. It's attractive. All the same——'

'All the same what, Mr. Bower?'

'All the same it all makes a tall story.'

'I'm sorry I can't shorten it for you.'

'Then,' he shrugged, 'I expect I'll have to accept it as the truth.'

Before she could answer that, tell him, as she fully intended to, that he could do what he liked with the story, he came in: 'So that's why you were late. You dallied at John's.'

'No. But John did show us the timber, the hops, the eucalyptus distillery, but the children going away as they did——' Too late she realized she had said too much. She closed her mouth, but knew it could not finish there.

'They went *where*?' he asked.

'They got bored with the distillery and went away.'

'*Where?*' Again he emphasized it.

'Away—I told you. Through the woods.'

'My God!' he exclaimed.

'It was, and is, all right. John's place backs into a mountain, there's no possibility of being lost.'

'But they were, I gather? You said they were late in coming back.'

'No. They met this man.' Again Jane stopped, knowing she had said too much.

'What man?'

'John knows him. A harmless old fellow.' As she said it Jane remembered Roberta's 'Not so old', but again did not dwell on it. 'He comes at times and lives with nature. I think' ... remembering Robert this time ... 'he's some sort of sculptor.'

'So eventually you rounded them up and returned here?'

'Yes. Mr. Donnelly told me about Wendy, and...' Her voice trailed off.

A minute went by in silence. It was a long minute. Then William Bower said: 'I thank you, anyway, for that, Miss Sidney.'

She nodded, and the silence started again.

'How did the kids go?' He broke the quiet. Evidently he had accepted her explanation, she thought, but how typical of the man not to admit it.

'Good. They're very applicable. Robert more than Roberta.'

'It's good to learn that the male sometimes leads,' he said drily. 'You believe then they both can be taught?'

'I'm sure of it. Robert is practically swimming already. Roberta——'

'Better follow suit. I've had word from the quarantine that the first contingent will be ready next week. Once they arrive you'll begin the duties you came here for.'

Jane said, 'Of course.'

'So if you can teach the children within five days——'

'I know I can.'

'Then' ... a narrow smile ... 'I'll forgive today's Johnny cakes.'

Jane said consideringly, 'I don't know whether it's your prerogative to forgive them or not.'

'In my employment time, it is.'

'And—out of employment time?'

'You mean before nine and after five? But a stablehand always should be available for emergencies, didn't you know that, or were the Little Down rules different, Miss Sidney?'

'The same. But I did have complete days off.'

'As you will have here.'

'And then, Mr. Bowers?'

'And then? Oh, of course, you mean is it my prerogative then?'

'I know it's not.'

'Then why do you ask me.'

'I didn't, I——' Suddenly Jane felt this was all too much, and she turned away.

But she turned back to ask: 'Was that all, Mr. Bower?'

'All, Miss Sidney.'

'Am I still to teach the children?'

'Still to teach them, Miss Sidney.'

'In five days?'

'Five days.'

'Good evening, Mr. Bower.'

'Good evening, Miss Sidney.'

Going into the big house, Jane passed Maureen sitting on the steps and polishing her boots. She was a pretty girl at any time, but she looked particularly pretty now, bent over the leather as she brushed assiduously, her long thick nut-brown hair touching her pink cheeks. No wonder Rodden——

'I'm not generally this funny, Jane,' she smiled, 'but my fellow's coming. That sounds like the hit parade, doesn't it? My Fellow's Coming.'

The second song in an hour. Johnny cakes with John had been the other.

'He's flying over,' Maureen went on. 'He's at Fetherfell across the Divide. Mr. Bower lets him have his second Cessna so he can flip over to see me. Oh, horrors!' She began removing boot polish from her ring. 'I shouldn't wear it when I'm working,' she grimaced, 'but it's very pretty, isn't it? It was bought in England.' She put her hand up to Jane.

78

Jane pretended to examine it ... well, she thought, what else could she do? She could scarcely say, 'I know it already, Maureen, you see it was my ring.'

She said: 'Yes, very pretty.'

As she left the girl she told her, 'Thank you for showing it to me,' but she really meant thank you for telling me Rodden is coming.

For when he arrives, she was thinking, I won't be here.

Her duties were over for twenty-four hours, except that self-appointed duty she had insisted Tim accept from her for the alternate feeding of Wendy's Pride. But she felt confident she could slip out unnoticed when she did that. Anyway, the small plane would not fly at night; Rodden either would be inside the house with his fiancée, or back at Fetherfell again.

She felt unhappy over her subterfuge with Maureen. She meant no deceit, she felt very attracted to the young strapper, but what else was there? She had to live with these girls. She wanted to live with them *amicably*. But no two women on earth, Jane thought, could live really amicably when one of them wore the other's ring. Then Kate, she considered, contemporary in age to Maureen, once ... or if ... she ever knew the truth, undoubtedly would support her friend. It was all very distasteful, but ... again ... what else was there?

She went down to the library that Bowers provided for all its hands and chose some books. Her first feed was at eleven, and she did not intend to sleep before that in case she really slept. Not ... tolerantly ... that Tim would criticize, he was no big boss.

The books she chose dealt with hop-growing and training a swimming champion. She smiled at her instinctive choice, then, hearing a craft circling over the house, from the sound of it a light craft, she wasted no time in taking the books upstairs.

She estimated that Maureen would ride out on the jeep to collect Rodden. Being lovers ... strange how that had no effect on her at all ... they would take their time to come in again. So Jane went down to the canteen at once for her evening meal. She met the nutritionist, several more of the hands, which was what she had wanted to do, but resisted their appeals, for in a male establishment like a stud it was almost an S.O.S., to stay on for some record playing.

She went upstairs again, lay down and read. She heard a light plane take off again just at last light, and knew that Rodden had left.

At ten she got up, put on her overalls, then went down the steps and out of the house. Across to the stud kitchen. She knew now where everything was, and she set to making Wendy's Pride's bottle with the same efficiency that she had made Turtle Dove's, Billy Boy's, Bella's ... half a dozen other's in her old strapper days. Back at Little Down, Rusty had always boasted that she was a dab hand on a bottle. 'We might even make a mother of you one day,' he had forecast. Jane smiled ruefully at that.

She had just finished warming it, and was testing it on the back of her hand, when the light in the kitchen went out. The plant was a local one, power had to be self-supplied up here, so either for conservation it was switched off at a certain hour ... she must remember next time to bring a lantern ... or it had failed.

Then a hand was gripping her shoulders, turning her round. But the hand did not stop her from crying out, a mouth did. A mouth pressed on hers.

In the small light from an outside lamp ... so nothing had failed, the darkness, like the mouth, had been deliberate ... Jane saw the outlines of a face—a man's face.

'Rodden!' she cried.

She pulled herself away. It was not so hard; evidently Rodden ... she knew a disgust ... had expected her co-operation, her participation, not her distaste, for he had not steeled his grip.

'Hi, what's this?' he demanded laughingly of her withdrawal. 'Going to play hard to get?'

'I'm not here to be "got" at all!'

'Oh, come off it, Janey, as soon as Bill Bower told me— very tactfully, of course, mindful of sparing me any more distress' ... a short laugh ... 'that you were coming out here, I knew what was in the wind.'

'If you were thinking——'

'I was.'

'Then you couldn't have been more wrong. I wouldn't come after you, Rodden, if——' She paused, not wanting to use old clichés but finding that this one filled her needs—'... if you were the last man on earth!'

'But you came,' he persisted.

'To look after the stock Rusty was sending out. Rusty was good enough to give me a share of them.'

'Yes, I heard about that,' Rodden said with interest. 'A fifth or something, wasn't it?'

'A fifth.'

'Anyway,' Rodden resumed, 'it was as good an excuse as any.'

'For what?'

'Janey, you used not to waste time like this,' he sighed.

'For what, Rodden?'

'Us, my dear girl. You've come to your senses, as I did, the moment I got back here.'

'The moment before or after Maureen?'

'Ah' ... evidently quite pleased that Jane had found out that she had not been indispensable ... 'I expected that.' As she did not comment, he went on, 'I can explain that.'

'I'm not interested,' she snapped.

'You see, darling, you were there but Maureen was here, and that, to a man, is the all-important factor.'

'Rodden, I'm not interested.'

'But Maureen is a wily witch, if she could have managed it she would have had it all down in writing, but the next best evidence was something on her finger. I didn't mind, there's more rings—and more girls—in the world, particularly one girl. You, Jane.'

81

'Rodden, can't you understand, I'm not interested in you.' But Jane knew she could not pretend uninterest in Maureen.

'Why have you built her up like this?'—'My fellow's coming,' Maureen, fresh young Maureen had carolled.

'Don't make a bête noir out of me—it takes two, remember.'

He was one of the most unpleasant men she ever had encountered. How on earth had she——

There were steps on the path that led to the stud kitchen. The light was still out, so it made Rodden's escape easy. Feeling absurdly heavy-hearted, though the heaviness, she knew, was for Maureen, Jane switched on the light just in time to catch William Bower turning the corner of the nearest building, then coming across to where she now stood at the door.

At the same time she saw that Rodden had left.

CHAPTER FIVE

WILLIAM BOWER looked at the feeding bottle Jane still held in her hand. 'You don't have to do this, Miss Sidney.'

'It's all right,' she insisted.

'You're not paid for it.'

'I'm doing it because I want to, Mr. Bower, because——'

'Love is ten cold nights in a paddock?'

'Wendy's Pride is in a cosy stable and it's a beautiful night.'

'Well,' he said, 'so long as Tim didn't ask you to.'

'Tim had to be persuaded to let me help out. He'll do the midnight and small hours and then I'll come on again at dawn.'

'Oh, no, you won't!'

'But the foal at this stage must have hourly feeds,' she protested.

'And will have, but not with you at the holding end of the bottle.'

'Tim has to have some rest—he told me that Persian Daughter is ready for her foaling at any moment and he believes it could be twins.'

'Yes, he has his hands full, and I wouldn't want him to forgo those few hours' sleep, but *you* are not doing it for him, Miss Sidney.'

'Why? I mean why apart from it not being my job at this moment?'

'Because,' he said frankly, 'you look done in.'

'Done in?'

'You look' ... he searched for a word ... 'concerned.'

Concerned ... she was more than concerned, she was terribly worried for Maureen. For a mad moment she felt like telling this man, asking for his advice. Then she remembered how concerned he had been in his turn—but for Rodden. You could say if there were sides, that William Bower was on Rodden's.

She said nothing, and after waiting a moment, perhaps for an explanation, but Jane could not tell from that enigmatical face, he said, 'Is the bottle ready, then?'

'I think I'd better warm it again, it might have got cold.'

'It couldn't have. I've only been here several minutes and you were coming out of the door.'

'All the same,' she evaded, and turning to the stove she quickly fixed it up to the desired temperature again. When she turned, he was still there. When she left the kitchen and went down to the stable, he went with her. Well, it was his filly, his stable, his stud.

There is nothing so appealing in the world, Jane thought a few minutes later, than a foal. Already Wendy's Pride had lost her wobble, but her not-quite-certain-yet spindle legs still could not judge distances, and when she came to meet Jane ... or the bottle, more probably ... she did it with that lovable awkwardness of all new young things. Jane gave her a taste of the goodies by putting her finger in the bottle and then in the filly's mouth. After which Wendy's Pride sucked deliciously. A little guidance, a lot of patience and a steady allotment of encouragement, pats and assurances, and Wendy's Pride soon was enjoying a good meal.

Jane had forgotten William Bower. Her preoccupation with the soft pansy-eyed thing so desperately dependent on her pushed everything else aside. It was almost with a start that she focused the man again.

'I'd forgotten about you,' she admitted a little foolishly.

He did not reply. *His* preoccupation had not been with the filly foal, so he had done no forgetting. He had stood watching her. It was with an effort, though he did not let her see it, that he took his glance away.

'Now back to the house,' he said a little gruffly. 'I'll see Tim and tell him I'll do your shifts. For that matter Rodden could do them—he flew in this evening and he's stopping the night. Bill Walsh, my pathologist, fortunately also a pilot, is taking the opportunity to see Fetherfell's bright lights.' He laughed—but cut short the laugh to ask sharply: 'Do you always flinch when you hear his name?'

'I don't know Mr. Walsh.'

'I didn't mean Bill, I meant Gair. Do you always flinch?'

'I didn't,' she protested.

'I assure you that you flinched. You better take a hold of yourself, Miss Sidney—if you flinch at his name, how will you be face to face?'

'I'll return the bottle to the kitchen and go to bed,' Jane said.

'*I'll* return it,' William Bower altered. 'Think over what I just asked you before you slip off to sleep tonight. I don't want you to lie awake, like an employer I want my money's worth from my employee, but some time or later you're going to meet up with Gair, and it's best to know ahead how you intend to handle that occasion. Because' ... a pause now, a warning one? ... 'he's betrothed.'—Betrothed, thought Jane a little hysterically. What a ridiculously old-fashioned word for a modern, sophisticated man!—'He's Maureen's now, and I wouldn't like any broken hearts to mend on this stud as well as our inevitable broken fetlocks and the rest.'

'But the human casualties are flown out, aren't they?'

'You know what I mean.'

'Yes, I do. But I don't think there'll be anything to mend.'

'I'd like your promise about that.'

'Mr. Bower, I'm tired,' Jane sighed.

'Your promise, Miss Sidney.'

'I promise, I promise, I promise! Will that do?'

'One would have done,' he asnswered, 'but said from the heart.'

'You're intolerable!' she flashed.

'You know what to do then?'

She followed his meaning. She asked coolly: 'How much would my one-fifth return me?'

'I'll tally it up, let you know in the morning.'

'Then I'll sleep on *that*.'

'As well as the other,' was his final advice. He stood back, let her pass him, then hurry up to the house. She had the fear that Rodden might not have returned to Maureen, that he might have been waiting behind some bush to see, and talk to, her again. She ran. She was breathless by the time she got to her room.

There she stood a long while at the window, thinking ... trying to find a solution.

She still had not reached any decision, when, suddenly recalling Bower's '... like any employer I want my money's worth,' she made at least one decision, and went to bed.

Jane made friends with Harry the next morning, apologizing over the untouched hamper, telling him how John had taken them to his house for hot cakes.

'Were they good cakes?' asked Harry jealously, and Jane grabbed her chance.

'Good, but nothing like your raisin scones, Harry.'

'I've put some into today's tuck, Miss Sidney, along with a slab of my cut-and-come-again. Lots of large places like Bowers, and certainly all projects, buy in big squares of sawdust instead of making their own cakes in their own kitchens. That's my name for it, sawdust, for that's what the tack tastes like. But not me. There's nothing like home-made, I say.'

'I say, too,' appeased Jane. 'Thank you, Harry, there won't be a crumb of this left.' She really intended that. No wandering off with John today.

As it happened, John did not come, but he left a message, Indian scout fashion, at the base of a tree.

The twins were enthralled tracking it down, and Jane thought what good father material John Rivers was for thinking of this. As far as she could see William Bower made no effort at all. He was a born bachelor. And yet, her thoughts ran on, he had looked furiously across his desk at her and called: 'My youngsters would be with me, and so, by heaven, would my wife.'—So sometimes . . .

'Here it is!' yelled Robert, who had first discovered the arrows on the ground and the mysterious 5 which meant, as all small boys know, 5 more paces. 'It's a letter,' he thrilled, 'for you, Jane.'

Jane smiled, took and read it. 'It's for all of us,' she announced. She read to her wide-eyed audience:

> *'Congratulations, Secret Three,*
> *At finding this beneath a tree.'*

This was a block of chocolate.

> *'I cannot join you, more's the sorrow,*
> *Let's hope for better things tomorrow.'*

'He's beaut,' awarded Robert.

'Jane's not,' pouted Roberta, seeing Jane take the chocolate firmly from them.

'It's strictly for swimmers,' bribed Jane. 'First one to do three strokes without my finger under their chin gets a block.'

Roberta won. She actually swam first. But Jane considered she would not advance very quickly from that level. On the other hand, Robert, like all boys seeing more danger, though slower to strike out, struck further and faster once he started. However, by hamper time they both could account for themselves for several yards, so Jane voted it a successful morning.

They ate every crumb from the hamper, as Jane had promised Harry, then the chocolate was split up, and the three lay back on the bank. It was unusual for Robert and Roberta not to be on their feet at once, exploring, discovering, but tracking the chocolate and, then earning the right to eat the chocolate had evidently exhausted them. The sun filtered down through the trees, the sand was a warm soft bed, the stream was a lullaby, and the two youngsters slept.

Jane dozed, too, but not as deeply as the twins, for she heard the jeep. She leaned up on an elbow to see William Bower sauntering across to the beach. As he came nearer she indicated the children, then put her finger to her lips.

He nodded, and she got quietly up and joined him.

'They look as though they're resting on their laurels,' he said.

'They are. Roberta did four strokes. Robert did six.'

'Excellent. I said five days, but I didn't expect——'

'In five days they'll be swimming the creek. Did you come down to see how they were progressing?'

'You didn't let me finish, Miss Sidney. I said five days, but I didn't expect you wouldn't have half that time. I've had a message from quarantine to get our first contingent out. I can't ignore it, room at Q is very precious. So we'll have to go up tomorrow.'

'And I'll start my real work.'

'I reckon you've been doing that here.' He said it sincerely.

Jane flushed with pleasure, she did feel satisfied with her results.

'I wouldn't like them to slip back, though,' she said regretfully.

'They won't. There's Maureen and Kate to fall back on. Maureen, for obvious reasons, has her attention across the Divide and not down the valley, but Kate would be quite keen, I think. She's a good swimmer, and would, I feel sure, like to carry on where you leave off.'

'Then that's fine,' said Jane. 'Can we collect the horses in a day?'

'Good lord, no, it will take three full days. One to get up there, two and three to get back. You can't eat up the miles with three horses trailing behind you as you can with only two aboard.'

'I see. So' ... a slight pause ... 'we have to stop overnight.'

'Two nights. One is Sydney, one night on the way back.'
He was looking in the children's direction with interest.
'Harry did you well for lunch, I see.'

She noticed that he was eyeing the chocolate wrapper,
which was a bright blue.

'I didn't mean to leave it there,' she assured him.

'Nor' ... a throaty laugh ... 'did someone else.'

'Someone else?'

'Don't move, Miss Sidney, but someone is about to take
up that wrapper.'

'There's no chocolate left.'

'He doesn't want chocolate, in fact he wouldn't know
what to do with it. He just wants blue.'

'Wants what?'

'Hush!' William Bower pointed, and, enchanted as the
children had been with John's game, Jane watched.

It was a shining, blue-black bird what William was indi-
cating, a glossy fellow with strikingly blue eyes. He did not
appear to pay any attention to them, but, William said
quietly, he would know they were there, he would have
looked them over to see if they offered anything blue. For
blue, Jane's boss informed her, was the bower-bird's obses-
sion. He pointed out the almost *compelled* way the bird was
approaching the chocolate wrapper, as though he *must* have
that flash of blue.

'Mind your blue eyes, Miss Sidney,' he advised.

Because of the bird's absolute absorption they could
speak to each other quite freely.

'Is it after this particular bird you named Bowers?' asked
Jane.

'Actually, no, this is a more rare specimen, it's the Satin
Bower-Bird, ours on the plateau is a more common variety.
But I did call the place Bowers for the birds as well as for
myself. I told you that.—Look, there he goes now.' The
bird, having darted down and lifted the wrapper, flew off.

'Do you know what,' said William, as excited as a boy, 'I
reckon his bower is in that thicket of bushes. It will be away

from his nest—they commute from nest to bower. Shall we look for it?'

'Will he mind?'

'Perhaps we can leave him something.' He glanced at the blue ribbon with which Jane had tied back her damp hair.

She removed it and handed it to him, her still-wet honey strands falling to her shoulders. She followed him into the thicket.

They found the bower at once. The bird had flattened down the grass to make room for his treasures, and the little square opened up as they parted the growth.

It was like looking into a tiny Eastern market, except that instead of many colours, all the purloined things were blue. Blue flowers. A blue river pebble. A discarded blue pen. Actually a blue dart that must have been taken from some camp and been rather awkward to carry. The new blue chocolate wrapper.

'It's wonderful!' Jane looked with delight on the flexible twigs with their ends stacked against each other, making a clear passage beneath the interwoven sticks to the previous spot.

'He may be returning with a heavy load,' said William, 'we'll not impede him.'

They stepped back. By the time they reached the river again, the twins were awake, and had to demonstrate their new art. Jane had intended to ask her employer to show the children the bower, but in their swimming pride, and her own pride for having helped achieve it, she forgot.

They went up to the plateau again, Roberta with William, Robert with Jane. As Jane went into the big house she met Maureen. The girl looked heavy-eyed today, all the sparkle of yesterday had left her. There was no 'My Fellow's Coming'. Kate was with her, and she loitered back when Maureen went off.

'Lovers' tiffs,' Kate sighed. 'I'm never going in for anything like that.'

'Sometimes it goes for you,' warned Jane.

'Well, it doesn't attract me. I think I'll settle for a borrowed family. Did Mr. Bower tell you I'll be taking over the twins and their swimming when you can't make it?'

'Yes. Thank you, Kate.'

'It'll be a change,' appreciated Kate. 'I've always loved the valley. I'm not a natural with horses, not like a strapper should be, I just took it on because I simply couldn't work at a desk and this was all that seemed offering. Well, I'll go and see to Maurie now. She and Rodden must have had a few words, because she never went out to the strip to wave him off again.'

'He's gone, then?'

'Oh yes.' Kate ran off, and, at a more leisurely pace, and in a much more relaxed state of mind, since Rodden Gair was no longer at Bowers, Jane followed.

The next morning, directly after breakfast, Jane and Willam left for Sydney. The three-horse float had been attached to the biggest of the Bower cars, and while the boss issued his stud orders for the next few days, Jane examined the float. Like all the Bower equipment it was ultra-modern and very functional. It also looked extremely comfortable. It was padded against bumps, roomy enough to let the passengers move away from each other, and weather-sound. Gretel, San Marco and Ruthven should enjoy a good trip down.

She waited beside the car and presently her employer joined her.

'Did you want to drive?' he asked.

'No.'

'You're entitled to, Miss Sidney. 'We're going after part of your possessions, so you have every right to see we arrive there safely to make the claim.'

'I believe we'll arrive safer in your hands—I don't know the road, remember.'

'It's a highway, once we get out of the valley.'

'How do we get out?' she asked.

'The track you take to the pool ... incidentally, the trio have already left! ... then along the flats to the coast. It's not as easy with this big car as with the jeep or mini, but you'll call it simple after you climb up from the valley again towing a parcel of horses. Oh, well' ... releasing the brake ... 'it makes us more exclusive up on top.'

They conversed idly until they had left the plateau and descended the valley, but once they had left the river, the children already there swimming with Kate and waving gaily as they passed, Jane turned her attention to the scenery, for this, for her, was new country. It as timber-land for a while, with occasional hop breaks, acres of apples, then gradually the lessening hills fanned out and down to softly-rolling fields that ran right to the sea. Mostly they were pea fields, their clean bright green contrasting with the bluest ocean Jane had ever seen. The sand was a warm gold, a contrast, Jane's driver told her, to the north coast, where the sands were creamy pale.

William Bower told Jane a lot of things on that trip, snippets of history, facets of natural life, all the outdoor things Jane always had loved, and all told in that robust manner that only an outdoor man who loves them, too, can tell. He showed her that he could be very charming as well as interesting and informative. Lunch at a restaurant overlooking a small south coast harbour became an event, not just a necessary restorative en route.

It was only when the coffee came that he struck the first discordant note.

'You asked me what your share would be worth, Miss Sidney.'

'Yes.' Jane was looking out at a cornflower blue sea and at the moment couldn't have cared less.

'I've been going through these two consignments, reducing them to the dollar state.'

'Yes,' Jane said again.

'It's not easy to give an accurate figure, one never knows with horseflesh if one has a champ or a miss.'

This time Jane murmured 'No', still looking at the sea.

'Gretel could prove a likely brood mare. Has she foaled much?'

'Once only. Quite successfully. A fine little girl ... I mean a filly.'

'I see.' His face did not alter at Jane's slip. He had taken out a notebook and he put down some figures.

'San Marco,' he said presently, 'I know already. According to racing news I've had sent out from England the fellow has a few country wins to his credit.'

'Yes, San Marco can sprint.'

'There's no reason why he shouldn't do it here.'

'He likes soft going,' warned Jane.

'I think you're trying to tell me he's a country horse—but *your* kind of country.'

'I was. I didn't mean any disparagement, I think I would love the country here. But not San Marco.'

'That's all right,' William Bower assured her, 'because, believe it or not, we can provide as gentle a terrain as your Surrey or Kent. And what's more, all with regular meets. In which case we can jot you down a nice figure for San Marco as well. Now how about Ruthven?'

'Not proved yet, but Rusty—but your uncle was very hopeful about him, he has excellent connections.'

'Then I'll strike an average figure for Ruthven.' William Bower did so.

He took out his pipe, called for more coffee, then said: 'That brings us to the second consignment.'

'The three D's.'

'Three D's ... oh yes, of course.'

For a few moments he attended to the ritual of packing, tapping and lighting, then he began.

'First of all, Dotsy...' He looked rather narrowly at Jane, though it could have been the smoke, she thought. 'We'll leave her last,' he said. 'Now, Devil May Care.'

'A winner,' came in Jane enthusiastically. She spoke proudly of how a young jockey at one of their northern

93

meetings had called in delight as he had raced Devil May
Care to first past the post the day before his marriage:
'You've just given me my wedding present, you fine boy!'

'He's tough, too,' she praised, 'and not at all tempera-
mental. I think Devil could even win one of your red earth
races.' As he jotted this down, Jane apologized a little un-
comfortably, 'I seem to be saying all good things. I hope
you don't think it's to—well——'

'To pop up the price? No, I don't think that. Anyway'
... an oblique look ... 'Dandy would bring the price down.
Miss Sidney' ... before Jane could indignantly interrupt
... 'why in tarnation did my uncle consign Dandy?'

'Dandy's a darling!' she exploded. 'Dandy ... why,
Dandy——'

'All right then, you love Dandy. Things like that happen.
I believe it's what they call a mutual look—— And why are
you looking at me like that?'

'Because—well, Rusty used to say that. He said if there's
a mutual look it will be all right.'

A silence had come between them. Jane, embarrassed,
kept her eyes to her cup.

'Did my uncle explain that phenomenon?' William
Bower broke the silence.

'He said,' Jane said a little unevenly, 'it was something
between the two of you and you two only.'

'I see. Do you know where it comes from?'

'The—look?'

'Yes.'

'No, I don't.'

'A man called John Keble wrote it. He said:

> *"Sweet is the smile of home, the mutual look,*
> *When hearts are of each other sure."* '

'I see,' said Jane.

He nodded. There was another silence. Then:

'But why in tarnation, why in Bower did he send
Dandy?' the man exploded. 'The boy—I mean the horse

94

has nothing. Oh, you've prettied him up. I've no doubt you've spent more hours on him than you have on yourself. All very nice, Miss Sidney, but when I jot Dandy down on the statement the profit goes down as well.'

There were so many rejoinders rising up in Jane. she could find voice for none of them. At last she almost croaked: 'All right then, get on to Dotsy. You said you'd deal with her last.'

'Can you take it?' he asked carefully.

'Take what?'

'What I'm going to tell you ... and what I think you don't know.'

Now Jane did look at William Bower. But she did not speak.

'I think ... mind you, I saw her only briefly in Sydney ... she's having a foal.'

'She is not!'

'And how would you know?'

'I'd know like I do with any of my girls, I mean—'

'Skip that. Keep on with how you'd know.'

'Well, she's agile.'

'She's early yet.'

'Slim.'

'The same reply to that.'

'I—I've watched her.'

'You'd want eyes at the back of your head. Look' ... a little more kindly ... 'I could be wrong. Anyway, we'll leave it for Tim and the experts. When Rodden's over, I'll ask him.'

It was just too much. Jane got up and left him to settle the bill. When he came out she was sitting in the car waiting to resume the journey.

He got in beside her.

'Not to be upset, Miss Sidney,' he tossed, 'it happens all the time. You can't cheat nature. Not' ... getting once more into the coastal road traffic ... 'after there's been a mutual look.'

'Can we just have the final figures without any comments?' Jane asked a few miles further on; it had taken her all that time to compose herself.

'Yes. The comment merely was made to prepare you for the lower sum you must be prepared to accept because of Dandy, who would line no pockets, also because of Dotsy, condition uncertain but suspected, and sire unknown.'

'I still don't believe you.'

'You may be right at that, it's not always easy to tell.'

'Also, if it's true, Rusty would know.'

'Then we must write and ask him, mustn't we?' He said it fatuously, knowing, she thought resentfully, that it would irritate her. 'The amount I've jotted down comes to ...' He told her a sum that positively rocked Jane. Never would she have put the value so high.

'One fifth of it would be——' he went on.

She disbelieved him for several minutes. It couldn't be that much! She couldn't be that rich. He must simply want to be rid of her.

'Mr. Bower,' she broke in indignantly, 'there's no need for bribery, no call for you to try to buy me out. If I wanted to go, I'd go, but not all the money in the world would hurry me.' She stuck out her bottom lip and finished, 'And *won't* hurry me!'

'I'm stating a correct sum, Australian-wise,' he said flatly. 'Perhaps you would get less in England where there's plenty offering, but out here where the top class commodity is more rare, you can almost name your own reward. So' ... negotiating a bend ... 'you don't want to leave yet?'

'I want to last out until the two contingents are settled, and I know that that's what Rusty wants.'

'All right then, we'll drop it. It was your idea, anyway, for me to give you a figure.'

'You've given it. Thank you.' Jane turned her head from him to look outside. They were still in the country, but closer settled country now. The space between the villages was considerably less. In half an hour the small towns seemed to have merged on each other to form an endless city.

'Yes, we're in Sydney,' Bower said when she commented on this, 'the outskirts now, but we'll make the hotel in a quarter of an hour.'

'What about the horses?'

'They can wait till tomorrow. But it will be an early tomorrow; we'll be taking off at daylight, and making it an easy trip.' He ran into a snarl of city traffic and did not speak again until they arrived and a porter collected the car to garage it, and, at Bower's indication, Jane followed another porter upstairs.

She was not tired, for it had been an easy transit; tomorrow with that 'we'll be taking off at daylight' of his, and the day after, should prove more strenuous journeys. She knew that William Bower had been hinting that she should rest to-night, and that any hint from Bower was tantamount to an order, but she had not seen Sydney before, only passed through it, and this fact as well as the rather exciting fact that she stood for more money than she had thought (even with the debits of Dotsy and Dandy, or so Bower said) made it impossible for Jane to stand still now. After she had showered and changed, she went to gaze down from the window to the city traffic below, at the canyons of streets between towering buildings, at a snippet of harbour that a slat of space separating two skyscrapers awarded her, and then, irresistibly, she turned and went down.

Inner Sydney was not such a big city, she found, since regional shopping and suburban spending had taken away from it, but the squares she did cover were exciting and comprehensive. Besides every London line she had loved, there was a subtle Eastern influence here, also the charm of flimsier, more tropical wear.

The fact that she stood for more money even though she did not have it in hand, made Jane more reckless than usual. She splurged on a pure silk blouse, a phial of brown boronia perfume and a wind-up jolly swagman who sang 'Waltzing Matilda' in a squeaky voice. Rusty would smile over him, she thought.

When she emerged from the souvenir shop, Jane knew she was lost. It did not bother her, for her hotel was a popular one and she could always ask ... but what did bother her was William Bower walking towards her. She determined not to let him know she had not marked the way she had come.

'So you've decided to sell out your fifth after all.' He was eyeing her purchases.

'I do have some money of my own,' she answered coolly.

'Finished now?'

'Yes.'

'Where to next?'

She thought hard. She wanted to see the quay and the Opera House. But she also wanted first to deposit her purchases. She took a chance and said: 'Oh, I'm just looking around,' and went down a side street.

He let her go, and it rather surprised Jane. He wouldn't want her company, she knew that, but it did appear to amuse him to have her by him for baiting purposes.

She hastened her steps ... then stopped, annoyed. It was a blind street. She turned back and found William Bower waiting for her, a grin on his face.

'Lost, aren't you?'

'No, of course not. I mean ... that is ...'

'Lost. Why won't you women note little details such as first turn to the left, second to the right? This way.' He barely touched her elbow with cool fingertips.

'Where are we going?'

'Where were *you*, apart from that looking around?'

'Well, I have these things—but I did think the harbour——'

She had barely got the words out than he had her in a store again, buying a carrier bag. Together they put in the parcels, then they took a bus to the quay. The Manly hydrofoil was ready to leave.

'It's a good way to see things,' said William Bower, helping Jane on.

Jane loved that harbour trip, loved the sails of the Opera House poised ready, one would think, for flight, loved the red roofs of the houses, the endless unfolding of little bitten-in bays all with their own golden beaches.

They had tea at Manly after walking to the ocean side, one long wave-kissed stretch of sand.

'You like the sea?' William asked as Jane poured.

'Yes. Only——'

He raised his brows in inquiry.

'Only I like "inside" the best,' she admitted, 'I like meadows, brooks, villages.'

'How do you judge paddocks, creeks, towns? As rather a bit too much, even though you say you like the "inside"? As too raw?'

'No,' she said, 'not at all.'

'Then does that mean you like our "inside" as well?'

'It's very beautiful,' she said sincerely.

'You'll see a different aspect of it tomorrow. We'll take the non-toll roads home for better scenery as well as less trammelled traffic.'

'After we get the fellows,' she said with anticipation; she had not thought she could look forward so much to seeing her contingent.

'Of course. That's our purpose.'

They left soon after that, returning this time by ferry.

'Want to see any more of Sydney?' Bower asked.

'Am I allowed?'

'I never said you weren't.'

'Then your words, Mr. Bower, emerge differently.'

'I'm glad you told me. I must watch myself when I say something I mean, otherwise you won't believe it. You never answered as to what you wanted to do.'

'The hotel,' Jane said, and got into the taxi he called over.

The next morning her summons to get up came with coffee. The maid told Jane that Mr. Bower said just coffee would do as they would breakfast afterwards on the road. Jane wasted no time and was downstairs almost on Bower's heels.

'Good girl,' he nodded.

They went direct to the quarantine, and there Jane went straight to the three D's, to talk to them, assure them it wouldn't be long now, to fondle Dotsy, pat Devil May Care, run her fingers round Dandy's soft ears. Dear, dear Dandy. And he, the great Bower, said the horse had nothing. Perhaps, in all honesty, Dandy hadn't, not if you put it down in figures, but he did have, Jane knew lovingly, a girl's heart. He had had it right from the beginning, ever since they had exchanged that mutual look.

'These three are staring daggers at you.' William Bower strolled across. 'Do you always play favourites?'

'They'll have me all the time now, but the D's won't, not for three more weeks.' She touched each D in turn. 'Be good,' she smiled.

Even after he had left the city traffic snarl behind them, William Bower drove moderately over the minor roads he had chosen. They took the Blue Mountains route, riding into soft blue air that changed to green at closer quarters, because that air, Bower told Jane, was coloured by distance from the wind turning over the eucalyptus leaves.

Then, the range conquered, they turned south once more. They lunched from a picnic hamper that the hotel had packed, and William Bower took out the horses and exercised them. Resuming south again, Jane noted fewer and fewer motels and inns, which was only to be expected, she thought, on a secondary road. She asked William where they would put up that night.

'A place called Iroola. It's comfortable and I can paddock the fellows. Not many motels or inns these days can accommodate horses as well.'

'That will be good for them,' Jane appreciated.

The travelled through the warm afternoon. Occasionally Jane napped. Then, at an ejaculation from the man beside her, she opened her eyes ... and gasped. It was now near elf light, the sun had gone down almost an hour, but instead of a last apricot flush, a first hint of dark pansy, the sky in front of them was charcoal, with, here and there, a streak of vicious red.

'Fire,' William Bower said. Even as they watched a dark smudge began spreading ominously, the blurred beginnings of a smoke pall to take over.

All the time William Bower kept driving, and thinking of bush fires of which she had read there were many in Australia, Jane asked shouldn't they stop.

'No. Never go back. Anyway, it's localized. It's no fire of nature.'

'How can you tell?'

'The shape of the pall. It could almost be an atomic explosion, couldn't it? No, it'll be a homestead.' he added, 'Poor devils.'

They drove for another half hour. It had become quite dark now, and Jane was concerned for herself as well as the horses. Where on earth on this dark smoky road were they to lodge?

As though he read her thoughts, Bower said: 'Iroola. I told you. Only a few minutes to go now.'

They did the last mile in silence. Jane knew that William Bower had grown as concerned as she was by the times he poked his head out of the window to try to pierce the gloom without the intervention of glass, by the occasions he sniffed deeply and estimatingly.

'It's close,' he said at last.

'The fire?'

'Yes.'

'Close—to us?'

'To the hotel.'

'You mean——'

'I mean I believe the hotel *is* the blaze. I only hope——'

101

She knew what he hoped, and she hoped with him.

Turning a corner, they both saw their hopes were in vain. All that remained of what once had been an inn was a smouldering ruin. Only a small annexe remained intact. Bower turned the car and float into a side track, drove some safe hundred yards, then told Jane to wait there.

He was a long time gone. Jane got out and talked to the horses, who seemed supremely unaffected, thank heaven, by it all, then she turned eagerly as she heard steps through the bush.

It was her boss again, and he gave her a reassuring smile.

'Bad ... but could be much worse. Not one life lost. The place is a shambles, but I have no doubt the Donnisons would be well insured. Mrs. Donnison is as cool as the proverbial cucumber ... how do you women do it? ... she even rang up Yanni for me—Yanni's further down—and got us a room.' He darted Jane the quickest of glances.

Only when they were on the road again did Jane recall that look. It came at the same time as she heard in retro-spect that '... got us a room.'

Us. Not you. Not me. And a room. Not rooms.

She opened her mouth. She shut it again. She moistened her lips.

'Yanni coming up,' said William Bower presently, 'no doubt the horses will be pleased.'

'No doubt.' Heavens, Jane thought, that was almost a croak.

William was going slowly now, it could be that they were almost at the place ... a very small place, Jane saw, strain-ing her eyes through the darkness ... or it could be——

'It's this way, Miss Sidney,' William Bower was saying.

'Yes?'

'In England do you have family units?'

'In hotels, you mean?'

'This is a motel.'

'I don't know. I mean——'

'Perhaps I'd better tell you what I mean, then. A family

102

unit is—well, for a family. It's larger than the usual accommodation. Generally quite a dormitory of beds. Well, to put it briefly that's all they have left. To put it more briefly still' . . . a pause . . . 'we have it.'

'We?' she echoed.

'We,' he said. And drove up to the door.

Mecahanically Jane helped him with Gretel, San Marco and Ruthven. She did the automatic strapping things that should be done to an animal which had been cooped up, even if it was in a roomy, comfortable box, for some hours. She fed, watered, brushed, massaged, soothed. Not that they needed soothing, they were perfectly calm and well adjusted.

Not like I feel, Jane thought.

At last she went to the room. A glance around the car-filled courtyard had assured her that it was in all truth a last offering, the motel was small, and, probably because of the fire at Iroola, now taxed to its limit.

The unit proved large, as William Bower had said it would be. There was a shower recess and its own kitchen. There were at least six beds.

'We could put quads in here as well.' William was standing at the door and looking across the room at Jane.

Suddenly Jane knew she had to say something . . . Anything at all would do. But what she could *not* do was to stay silent. And meet his eyes.

She began to chatter. Shocked at her nervous babble yet somehow unable to stop herself, she agreed: 'Yes, we could put up a whole family, couldn't we? Which bed for you? I'll take this. I'll shower and then you can. I'll . . . you'll . . . we'll . . .'

At last she found she could stop, and she did.

He was still looking at her, but differently now.

'Don't waste your breath,' he advised. 'But do have that shower.'

'I——'

'The shower, Miss Sidney.'

103

His eyes compelled her, she didn't want to go, she wanted to calm herself, to be matter-of-fact, sensible, practical, a woman of the world, a girl of today, not the—well, the near-hysterical ninny she was being now. But she went.

When she came out again from the bathroom, he wasn't there. Jane got into her selected bed and shut her eyes. Around ten o'clock, she judged, the motel electric plant cut out, and the light she had left on for him switched off.

She listened for him, but did not hear him. She listened ... listened ... Then she was opening her eyes to the first pale buttering of piccaninny daylight ... and at once turning those eyes to the rest of the dormitory beds. They were all still closed up. No one had slept there.

Jane dressed rapidly and went out to the courtyard. The car was where it had been last night, and the float beside a shed that they had been given for a shelter for the horses.

She went to the barn and looked in. Gretel, San Marco and Ruthven looked back, and San Marco whickered. She glanced around, but saw nothing—and nobody—else. Then that must mean that the motel had found William Bower a room after all. She was glad about that, but felt he could have come back and told her.

As she came out of the barn she had a feeling that someone was watching her. She hesitated, then looked to the car ... and saw that it was William Bower. As she looked back, he yawned, stretched and heaved his big person from the back seat.

'Sleep well?' he asked her.

'Yes.' Jane hesitated. 'Did you?'

'No. Ever try a fitted box?'

'You needn't have slept there, Mr. Bower.'

'I know,' he nodded. Then he mimicked cruelly : 'Which bed for you? I'll have this one. I'll shower and then you can.'

'What,' broke in Jane in anger, 'did you want me to say?'

He regarded her with cool estimation. 'Ever consider trying the truth?'

'You must have read it even though I didn't say it,' she flung, 'by coming out here.'

'I came out here because I preferred out here, because I have no time for humbug. Why in heaven couldn't you have said: "Bower, I will not sleep in a family unit if you're there, I know it's the only thing offering, but it's not for me." Why did you try to slide out like you did?'

'I didn't, I——'

'You floundered and dithered and generally made me sick, Miss Sidney. Either you wanted me *not* there or you wanted me *there*, but you were too "nice", too "polite"— and too damn puerile to say it!'

'Then I'll say it this time,' said Jane. '*I did not want you there.* As for the other possibility, that——'

'Wanting me to remain?'

'As far as that's concerned, I'm now *not* too nice, too polite, too puerile to tell you that that would be the very last wish I could ever make, Mr. Bower!'

'How soon' . . . frozenly and finally . . . 'before we push off?'

CHAPTER SIX

AT mid-afternoon, when they reached the Urara valley, Jane leaned out to wave to Maureen and the twins, who again were swimming in the creek, but William Bower did not stop, presumably since he had a tricky run in front of him to gain the plateau, but more probably, Jane thought feelingly, because he was still in that filthy mood.

They had barely spoken since they had left last night's hotel. They had eaten lunch in near-silence at a roadside teahouse, then resumed the return journey just as silently. The man did not even acknowledge the children as they crossed over the small bridge. He made it seem as though driving the float on this final lap needed all his attention, and perhaps it did, but all the same ...

It was so unfair of him, Jane's mind ran on resentfully. Perhaps she *had* babbled too much, been a fatuous little fool, but the unit had taken her by surprise. He had. She saw now that she had marked something that was really nothing at all by dithering over it, but good heavens, not everybody was as cool, as certain of themselves, as supremely composed as he was.

If she could have explained now, she would have, but she still had no words, and ... a surreptitious glance at her driver ... no reception.

As they ascended, in all fairness Jane had to excuse William Bower's absorption. The hairpin bends, the tortuous curves were all in a day's work to her mini model, but for a big car towing a float it was a hard, hazardous trip. But at last they were on the top and travelling the last miles to the stud.

William Bower drove up to the stables. 'I'll get a couple of the boys to help me unload them,' he tossed, 'settle them in. You can knock off.'

'No, thank you.'

'That was not a consideration, Miss Sidney, it was an order. You've had a long day.'

'So have you. And I' ... getting a word in at last ... 'at least had the benefit of a good night's rest.'

'I didn't. But I'm still signing you off.'

'I'm not going. After all, I'm a partner, not an employee in this.'

He looked thunderous a moment, but he must have seen he would have to climb down.

'All right then, do the chores yourself. I'll send Andy and Bert along.'

'We don't need four for three horses.'

'I'll sign myself off. No need for everyone to be tired.'

About to retort, 'I'm not,' Jane left it at that.

After Andy and Bert had got Gretel, San Marco and Ruthven out and into their boxes, Jane still stayed on. She brushed them, cosseted them, watered them, fed them, extending each chore unnecessarily. She knew she was filling in time, but she had to work off her frustration.

It was dark when she came out at last. It was several hundred yards to the big house, and Jane looked across to the twinkling lights rather nervously. Had Rodden come again? Was he likely to step out at one of those shrubs? And yet it was what she really should strive for, another meeting, but this time with a definite understanding, with Rodden.

She forced herself to walk calmly, not hurry as she had before, to the house. But Rodden did not step out, and when she entered the building he was not there either.

After dinner she sat in the common room and listened to records. The men obviously enjoyed her company, particularly as tonight neither Kate nor Maureen were there. Kate, they reported with malicious glee, was child-worn; that should learn her, trying to get a family the easy way! Over Maureen, they were more serious. It was strange, Jane thought, how in a small community individual troubles became public cares. Maureen didn't look happy, they said, and for a while they looked unhappy themselves.

Feeling false, Jane made the suggestion of pre-wedding jitters.

'But Maureen's not being married for ages,' said the nutritionist.

Tim, the vet, added: 'She's a damn pretty girl, I can't understand what's holding Gair up.'

'I suppose after his last experience——' murmured someone.

'First I've heard of a man being a jiltee,' said someone else. 'Is jiltee a word?'

They argued amicably, and pleading weariness after a long day Jane went upstairs.

She regretted that at first when she reached her room. Maureen was sitting at the window.

'I'm sorry,' the girl said. 'I shouldn't have come in.' She shrugged. 'But I did.'

'That's all right, dear. I'm glad you're here. Tea?'

'No. That is ... All right, then.' A pause. 'Jane——'

Jane switched on the jug before she turned. She made herself do that.

'Yes, Maureen?'

'You're always so calm.'

'I think calmness is something a strapper acquires, you have to be calm with horses.'

'I'm a hand, too, but——' Again the girl was quiet a moment. 'Jane——'

'Yes, dear?'

'I can't ask Kate, she's younger than I am, only a few months, but—well—— Not that you're much older.'

'Almost five years, Maureen.'

'Is it five? It doesn't seem it, I mean not just in looks, but—well, in the *way* you look.'

'How do I look?'

'Not unhappy. Not ever. But then you haven't been in love, have you, Jane?'

108

'Love shouldn't make you look unhappy.' Jane hoped Maureen did not notice she had not answered her question.

'It does me. I know you can't help me, but Kate is quite hopeless. All she says are things against Rodden—she doesn't like him, never did—but it can't be all Rodden, can it, some of it must be me. My fault, I mean.'

'Some of what?'

'The change in him. The——' A pause, quite a long one now. 'Jane, I don't think Rodden wants to marry me.'

'But, dear, you have his ring,' Jane heard herself say, and was a little shocked at her duplicity.

'His ring . . . or someone else's? I think that sometimes. I don't know why. Jane . . . Jane, what's gone wrong? Oh, I know you can't say, you wouldn't anyway, you're too sweet. But I just had to blurt all this out to someone, not to young Kate who would only say "Ditch him". I—I won't have that tea after all. Thank you, Jane.'

She was gone before Jane could protest.

Jane did not have tea, either. She went and sat where Maureen had sat, by the window. Most of the lights had been switched off before she went to bed.

A few days from a stud made a big difference. Jane had found that out in Little Down. She supposed it was nature; nature never stood still. In the short period she had been away, Persian Princess had foaled. She had come through wonderfully, Tim reported to Jane, for a mother of twins. Maureen, he added very warmly, had been a marvellous help. But the little fellows, a colt and filly, seemed to be slipping back. Tim asked Jane to attend and see what she thought.

Jane had had no experience in this. Rusty had had a twin birth, but it had been the mother who had looked ill, though eventually she had recovered. This mother, Persian Princess, obviously was in perfect condition. But the two foals . . . Maureen, kneeling by them, looked up at Jane and shook her head sadly.

The girls between them 'specialed' the foals all that day. Jane thought several times of her own three, and whether they were feeling strange and abandoned, but she put the thought aside. At least they were fit and had each other. These poor small mites . . .

If nothing else, the watching of the foals diverted Maureen, but seeing the end in sight Jane wondered whether she would have been better without such diversion, for it would be harder now.

It was. When the foals died late in the afternoon, Maureen broke up in a quite unprofessional manner. There were floods of tears. The girl was near-hysterical. Tim came forward and took the distraught Maureen in his kindly arms. Jane hesitated, wondering if she should offer her comfort, too, but decided to leave it at that.

She went out to the stable.

William Bower was crossing to it, and to spare Maureen, though Jane had a suspicion that Maureen would have got off lighter than she, Jane, would have in the same circumstances, Jane went forward.

'The foals died,' she said.

He nodded. 'I expected it. Bad luck. But better for the poor little atoms to go now if there was something gravely amiss.'

'I believe there was,' said Jane.

'We'll have Tim do a post,' William decided. 'It may have been that two births upset the result for Princess where one would have been a routine affair, or it may be that she just isn't a breeder.'

Still Tim and Maureen did not emerge. 'I was going to see Persian Princess,' Jane said to give Maureen more time to compose herself.

'To break the sad news.' William was lighting his pipe and his smoke-narrowed eyes baited Jane.

She looked at him coldly. 'She may be very uncomfortable; Tim said there was enough milk for two.'

'I'm sorry,' he offered at once. He really did seem

ashamed of himself. 'I didn't mean to needle you, not on a thing like that. The Princess does have a lot of milk. But I believe we can fix that. Rodden lost a mare while we were away over at the Fetherfell stud' ... he frowned and was quiet a moment ... 'and is badly in need of a foster for the orphan.' They had turned into Princess's box now.

The mare did look at a loss, and Jane said: 'I think what you suggested would be wise, I believe you should make her a foster.'

'We'll go over tomorrow, then, I'll take the Cessna and we'll bring the orphan back.' He touched the silky nose. He looked worried, Jane considered, and she felt she understood. Running a stud, she remembered from Rusty, could bring many worries, though she hardly had believed that this self-sufficient, efficient man ...

Her silence must have started something. 'I lost another one today.' Bower's voice actually shook slightly.

Jane remained silent.

'Cam was an old friend,' he said presently, 'quite ancient. I expect a man is a fool to——' He shrugged.

'He died?'

'I had him put down. He was crippled with rheumatism, I couldn't see him suffer another season.'

Jane nodded.

'Well, that's the way it goes.' William Bower broke the small silence. 'How are your three?'

'I really haven't had time to look into that.'

'You should, you know. Anything apart from them is just employment to you, not personal property.'

'One-fifth of,' she reminded him.

He ignored that. 'See to your own interests,' he advised briskly. 'Don't consider anyone else.'

Jane wondered if her sympathy because of his departed mate that had been trembling quite apparently on her lips had caused his sudden brusqueness. Possibly this withdrawn man had resented her intrusion. She stiffened herself. 'Always think of Number One,' she interpreted. 'Yourself first.'

'Exactly,' he nodded. Then he nodded to Jane and went back to the house.

The next day they flew over to Fetherfell. Scarcely were they up than they were descending again, gradually lowering to the green slopes of the tablelands, that stretched, William Bower called out to Jane, right to the plains, and then, given time, to Australia's red centre. But at Fetherfell it was green and rolling, not red, and, coming after the sudden and dramatic abyss that separated it from Plateau, very peaceful as it looked back and up at them. It was a comfortable-sized hamlet, William also called, a hospital, several streets of shops and a railway station. Jane, woman-like, was a little regretful she would not be seeing the shops, but she had to accept that fact as William flew the Cessna across the town, then put the plane down in a wide paddock strategically marked for take-offs and landings by white up-turned plastic buckets. They must be at the satellite stud. Shortly after their arrival a jeep came out. Rodden drove it, and Jane stiffened herself, not because it was Rodden she was about to encounter a second time, but because on this occasion she would have an observer. And of all observers, William Bower.

She pitied herself as the jeep drew up. It was two against one, she thought childishly, for William Bower's sympathies were entirely with Gair. She stood and waited.

Then she was sensing a rather strained atmosphere between the two men. Rodden greeted his employer as an employee would, but there was a challenge there. William was almost terse.

They got into the jeep. They went at once to the stables, and while Jane fussed over the small orphan, the men went out to the yard. It was soon afterwards that she heard William's raised voice.

'Two of them! Good lord, Rodden!'

'It happens.' Rodden's voice was lower, but still clear to Jane's ears.

'Is that all your explanation?' demanded Bower. 'That it happens?'

'I'll make my report, of course, but I'm not Mother Nature, or Father, either, sir.' The sir was almost flung at William, thought Jane. 'Also I don't play Fate and pull strings as to who survives and who doesn't.'

'But two in as many days!'

'It happens,' Rodden repeated.

'I suppose I'll have to accept that, but I'll still study your report.'

'In professional terms or for laymen?'

'I don't want your impudence, Gair.'

'I don't want it, either, but it appears to me that you're questioning my skill.'

'No. I know your skill. But I could question your management.'

'And are you questioning it now?'

'Look, we'll leave it this time. Persian Princess lost her twins.'

'Then in a way this misfortune is opportune.'

'Misfortune is never opportune, don't ever try to rationalize that it is. But because I haven't time, I'll close the subject here. Miss Sidney——'

Jane, who had moved to the door of the barn for better listening, gave a guilty start, then went out.

'Mr. Gair has just broken the news that we have two foals to succour, not one, that two mares went down. This means that both foals will have to go over to Bowers, and it means also that there'll be no room in the larger Cessna for you. Mr. Gair will return you in the smaller craft.'

'Yes, Mr. Bower,' Jane said.

Rodden led the way to the second orphan, then the two tiny foals were carried to the jeep, after which Rodden drove William Bower and his cargo out to the waiting craft. With minutes the Cessna was taxiing off, then turning into Plateau's direction again. Jane saw Rodden coming back. He was in a bad temper, which at least diverted his atten-

113

tion from Jane, even though the effect would only be temporary.

'Glenda was too old,' Rodden said angrily. 'What did he expect me to do? Perform a miracle? These laymen!'

Jane had heard that said to Rusty, and it was Rusty she defended when she answered, 'Sometimes experience is a better thing than an instruction in a book.'

'Oh, so we're all for the boss now, are we?'

'No. But I can see his point. What happened?'

'They both died foaling, that's all. As I said, it happens.'

It did happen, knew Jane, but not generally so frequently. She thought of old Cam, who had had to be put down, of the twin foals who had died, and now, on top of these losses, the added losses of two mares. She explained it to Rodden.

'When do I cry?' he said.

'Rodden!'

'Sorry, my beautiful, I do say the wrong thing, don't I? I should have remembered.'

She knew what he meant, he was referring to the Little Down Melinda incident, and she put in quickly: 'That's all over.'

'The ashes are not white yet,' Rodden reminded her.

'They are for me.'

'I don't believe you, Janey.'

'Besides,' said Jane, 'there's Maureen.'

'Yes. There's Maureen,' Rodden said slowly, thoughtfully. Then: 'Thank you, Jane.'

She looked at him in surprise, surprise that he had accepted her reminder so calmly. She felt she had never known Rodden.

'Well,' he shrugged, 'we'd better get going. How do you feel entrusting your life this time to me?'

'Presumably you can fly,' said Jane.

'I can.'

The smaller craft was garaged in a hangar on the field. It was very light and only needed help from a stablehand to

114

wheel it on to the path. At Rodden's nod, Jane climbed in, then Rodden climbed after her. The engine whirred, the small machine went forward, and they nosed into the air.

Coming across, it had seemed to Jane that barely had she looked down on the valley beneath Plateau than she had been looking down on the tablelands of Fetherfell, but evidently, perhaps because of its smaller size, this craft must take longer than those few minutes, for already they had been up for a lengthier period, and the stud still was not in sight.

Peering over, a little puzzled, Jane caught the different note in the engine. She glanced at Rodden, but he did not look back. She looked down again, and saw that they were approaching a clearing in a valley.

'Rodden, you're landing,' she called.

'Looks like it, doesn't it?'

'But why?'

'Fuel, lack of, is the usual accepted excuse,' he replied. 'I'll be reprimanded, no doubt, about that, but oh, what manna from heaven!'

'Rodden, what on earth are you talking about?'

'Shut up, Jane, there's no buckets to mark the way here.' All the same he landed, and landed perfectly. He was good, she had to admit. When the small plane finally stopped, he sat back and looked at Jane.

'Thank you, Jane darling,' he said.

'For what?'

'For saying that, for reminding me, "There's Maureen."'

'What do you mean, Rodden?'

'You may be a good strapper, Janey, but you're not good at catching on. I mean us, of course.'

'How, Rodden? Why?'

'How? By Maureen not caring about this little episode.' He slid ... or tried to slide ... an arm around Jane. 'Why? because it's you, Jane. It was. It is. It will be. Anyway' ... as Jane pulled right away now ... 'it's not Maureen.'

'How will this make a difference?' Jane was looking at

115

the isolation of the valley strip and feeling more hollow than she would have cared for Rodden to know.

'Darling, you shock me.' Rodden had taken out his cigarettes.

Flippantly . . . or she tried for flippancy . . . Jane yawned: 'All that went out years ago, Rod. You're being very naïve.'

He exhaled lazily. 'I admit that the scheme is a trifle old-fashioned.'

'It's antiquated!'

'But' . . . ignoring Jane . . . 'it still has its points. Maureen, for all her flaming youth, isn't so flaming after all. I'd even go as far as to say she's slightly Victorian, and that she won't like this.'

Jane stared at him in loathing. However had she felt anything for this man?

'Why can't you tell her outright?' she demanded.

'I could,' he said, 'with your support. If you would come with me and say——'

'I wouldn't.'

'Then' . . . a shrug . . . 'we have to adopt measures.'

'Don't include me.'

'Janey, the whole procedure is because of you.'

'You're crazed, Rodden, you must be! You know as well as I do that it's all over, why otherwise would I have sent you the ring?'

'In a fit of pique,' he suggested, 'because I wouldn't dance to your tune. Hushabye, Baby, wasn't it? Belinda's baby?'

'Melinda,' Jane said mechanically.

He ignored her correction. He said what she had expected him to say. 'You followed me out.'

'Rodden, I never followed you out! I came because——'

'Yes, you've said all that before. But the fact still remains, Janey, for everyone's . . . and Maureen's . . . consumption that we were once engaged, that we split up, that

116

I came home.' A deliberate pause. 'That now we're together again.'

'We are not!'

'Aren't you forgetting something?' He glanced significantly around him, and she followed his meaning. They *were* together, as together as two people in a lonely valley, miles away, she expected, from anything had to be.

'It makes no difference,' she said firmly.

'To you, perhaps, but—Maureen?'

'She's young, and the young are outgoing, not—not vulnerable in things like that any more.'

'Don't you believe it. How would you like your fiancé away all night in the bush with a beautiful girl?'

'I won't be away all night, Rodden.'

'Then you'll still clinch it, darling, for sure. If you're found scratched and bedraggled by running through the undergrowth from me, everyone will think the worst.'

'Of you, Rodden.'

'That will do nicely, thank you. My little Maureen, who is sweet, I'll admit, but as cloying as sugar, will be handing back your ring in flash.'

'It is *not* my ring!' she snapped.

'I agree with you there entirely, Jane, we'll start off anew, start another life with another stone. What will it be?' he smiled.

'Aren't you being rather reckless, jeopardizing, or trying to jeopardize, your career with the Bower stud like this?'

'I'm not just trying, Jane, and no, I don't think so. Bower and I are all washed up, anyway. Those damned mares——' He scowled. 'I can get a job anywhere, Jane,' he went on. 'With your little capital we two should——'

'My little capital is staying with me, Rodden.' She looked at him contemptuously. 'Is that the reason——'

'No. No, Jane. It's just as I said: it's you. *You*. Maureen has been bothering me for some time. The old, old story' ... a laugh ... 'she wants to proceed from the ring.'

'It's customary,' Jane observed.

117

'But it wasn't for you. You never pursued, did you? Not until now.'

'*Not* now, Rodden, please try to realize that.' She actually leaned across to him. '*Know it*, Rodden,' she advised.

Something must have penetrated, for Rodden sat quiet a while.

'You'll change,' he said presently, 'and at least it will get Maureen out of my hair.'

'If she learns.'

'Of course she will learn. Even by now Bower is allotting me another black mark for running out of fuel, and as you must know by now, that man never does things by halves. Undoubtedly the mechanic knows, and from the mechanic the next down, or the next across. Right across to the stables? I think you can say, Janey, that when we don't arrive by dusk, everyone will be aware.' A small pause. 'Including Maureen.'

'You're hateful!' she burst out.

'Yet efficient?' He had taken out another cigarette.

'I don't know.' Jane was narrowing her eyes to the further end of the clearing. There was no road from the small valley strip, but there must be a track of sorts, for a jeep was labouring up. She heard Rodden give an angry grunt.

'They're coming across,' Jane said unnecessarily, for she knew that Rodden would be equally aware of that.

She wondered who it could be ... some bushman who had seen them put down and suspected they were in trouble? Surely not William Bower himself, there would not have been time.

Then she heard shouting, and began to laugh. For, as opposed to Rodden's two of them, it appeared there were to be six of them. John drove the jeep. Kate sat beside him. Behind them both sat the twins.

'A ring from Bowers,' John called. 'Bill Bower reckoned you'd be putting down here, and he was right. He told me to bring out some gas for you to get back to Fetherfell,

118

Gair, but for us to fetch Jane.'

John helped Jane down, then, with a big white handkerchief, flagged Rodden out of the valley again. It was not so difficult, the craft was small and the cliffs banking down to the valley were in accommodating positions.

It was only when the plane had gone that Jane noticed that Rodden had *not* taken on any fuel. She hoped that John did not notice that the supply he had fetched out had not been touched. That if he did, later, he would not be sufficiently interested to tell William Bower. Yet did Bower need to be told?

'Bill reckoned you'd be putting down here,' John had said.

Just as he seemed to know everything, even the biological condition of Dotsy, it appeared that the great Bower had also known this.

But William Bower said nothing at all. All the way up to the stud, Kate driving the mini that had been parked in front of John's when they had emerged from the valley strip ... more Johnny cakes? Jane wondered briefly ... Jane had rehearsed her answers to Bower.

But there had been nothing to answer to. Neither had any of the innuendoes, subtleties and sarcasms she had anticipated been voiced.

'There's been a hitch in the fostering,' was what the stud boss said instead. 'It appears that the Princess isn't as well endowed as I thought, and can only provide for one orphan. However, as you already have a hand-feed job, Miss Sidney, Maureen will take over our second waif.'

Jane nodded ... and still waited. He was not the kind of man to let a thing like this pass.

But he did let it pass, and because the boss did, all the stud did, too. No doubt they had noticed and noted Gair's non-arrival after Bower—working almost on the landing paddock as they did they couldn't help being aware—and no doubt, too, they had noticed and noted Jane's arrival by car instead, but there was no question, no comment. Jane

119

accepted it thankfully, she had been dreading the construction Maureen might put on the brief episode. As it was, it had been so brief that it became no episode at all. Jane liked Maureen, and she wanted no change in their friendly relations.

There was no change ... not apparently. Maureen asked Jane for her formula for feeding. She asked several other pertinent questions. It was as if nothing had happened. And yet ... Jane could not put a finger on it, she did not even know why she thought it, Maureen was as pleasant and as nice to know as ever, but somewhere there was a withdrawal. She could be imagining it, Jane told herself, but there was no outgoing any more from the younger girl to Jane. It was a pity. That night she had opened her bedroom door and found Maureen there had been a very precious moment, Jane knew in retrospect. A younger girl coming to an older one is always an intrinsic thing.

But it was not like that now. Maureen, though she sought Jane out, asked for advice, nodded agreement, thanked Jane, *all the time looked away*. Had she not found herself suddenly very busy, Jane could have fretted over that.

Her first consignment was now entirely in her care, and the seven weeks they had been out of training would take some catching up, Jane soon found. Gretel had put on weight and needed exercise to reduce that tub she had achieved; San Marco, who had won several country events in U.K. and had revelled in activity, had grown lazy, and Ruthven of the good connections was only showing outward signs of the bad sides of his families.

'You slackers are going to wake up,' Jane said sternly.

That week went as though it was a day. As soon as she was off Gretel, Jane was on San Marco, San finished she tackled Ruthven. They protested at first, they had become used to the *dolce vita*, but slowly they sniffed the old sweetness of dew-wet, herby-breathed morning paddocks (for meadow or paddock the sweetness was still the same) and the indolence they had got into dropped away. They became Jane's fellows again.

She was exhausted every evening, and sometimes she nearly fell asleep over the feeding of Wendy's Pride, who was coming along very nicely, and making the second hand-fed orphan, Billy Boy, attended by Maureen, look very junior indeed. Jane wondered how the lucky foal who had won himself a mother and not an attendant with a feed bottle was faring, and went out to the east paddock where Persian Princess and Little Persia, as the adopted foal had been named, were domiciled.

When she reached the sliprail, she stood and laughed. Persian Princess was every inch a princess. Her mother had been a queen, Jane had learned, Queen of Persia, her sire something equally regal. The Princess moved haughtily, even when she cantered it was with royal dignity. But now a lot of the protocol was wiped out, wiped out by a rather shaggy, ridiculously spindly-legged, mischievous, distinctly plebeian bundle of colthood, name of Little Persia, rollicking by her side. They just didn't match, that pair, the top drawer mother, the bottom drawer baby, and when they ran together it was almost buffoonery. Jane laughed till the tears came to her eyes.

'And yet,' pointed out a voice at Jane's side, 'the Princess is as proud as Punch, or as proud, anyway, as if she had her own elegant offspring beside her, not the product of Scaramouche out of Ragamuffin.'

'Is that the baby's line?'

'Yes.' It was William Bower who had joined Jane.

'Little Persia wouldn't change mammas either,' Jane said, smiling at the odd couple. 'It's strange, when they're so unlike.'

'It must be that mutual look that did it,' he offered, "... when hearts are of each other sure."'

'I rather think it's a sure meal as far as Little Persia is concerned.'

'How factual we are today!' William looked at Jane more closely. 'Or is it weariness making you see only the

121

business side? I've been watching you, Miss Sidney, you really are working your fellows hard, aren't you? What's the incentive? Is it because they personally belong?'

'Only a fifth of them. No, not entirely. They were in shocking condition.'

'Were?'

'I believe they've improved.'

'I believe so, too. I was looking them over'—Jane fumed privately at that, but had to add in all fairness that he had every right to, he owned more of them than she did.

'Yes?' she asked.

'Gretel is losing her tub.' A sly pause. 'Easier to get rid of it, I would say, than Dotsy's.'

'*You* are saying that, Mr. Bower, I'm not. Not yet.'

'Have you written to my uncle asking him?'

'I will.'

He nodded, and resumed once more.

'San Marco looks fine. So does Ruthven. Which brings up a subject I would like to discuss.'

'Yes, Mr. Bower?'

'I'd like to try those two fellows out at a few meets. How does your one-fifth feel about that?'

'Four to one doesn't give me much scope to feel anything,' Jane said.

'That's a different story from what you boasted before, then your fifth had the final say. Seriously, though, would you have any objection?'

'Of course not. I want them to race. It's what Rusty bred them for.'

'There's a few provincials coming up, I'd like to try out their reaction.'

'How do you mean? They've both raced before.'

'Try their reactions to the various courses, which you'll soon see down here can be categorized as good, medium, then problem, or poor. I don't know how it is over in U.K., but in some of our more inferior backgrounds there are still some excellent prizes offering. Also, though the going is

122

rough, some horses actually like it rough.' William Bower looked at her.

'Yes, I believe Ruthven could be one,' mused Jane, 'though I don't know how rough.'

'We can try them out, gradually lessening the standard of fields. I may as well tell you now what I'm really after. I'd like finally to enter one, or the two, of them in the coming Farley Downs event.'

'Downs don't sound rugged to me,' she commented.

'Your downs mightn't, but these are in our red centre, and more sand and spinifex than turf.'

'Oh,' Jane said.

'Anyway, think it over while we do the preliminary trials. There's a meet on Friday at Lilyborne, down the coast, a very pretty, very green picnic race sort of place, that I'm sure you'll like as well as San Marco and Ruthven. It won't be so much different from your own plusher courses. After we get over Lilyborne we'll ... but one thing at a time, the next can wait.' He looked at her. 'Yes?'

'Yes,' Jane agreed.

As taking the horses down to Lilyborne would entail an entire day and an early start, Jane asked Maureen to take over the feeding of Wendy's Pride. Maureen already had the Fetherfell foal in her care, but she agreed at once ... yet still, Jane somehow felt, with that slight withdrawal.

'Maureen,' she wanted to say, 'what is it? Can't we sort this thing out?'

But almost as if she anticipated something, the younger strapper assured her: 'Don't worry, Jane,' and left Jane standing and watching her go. *And worrying.*

It was useless asking Kate, who was so enthralled in her twin-minding and valley excursions that Jane wondered how she would take to stabling again when the children's parents returned, so Jane just let it pass.

The take-off down to Lilyborne was to be very early, and it was still dark when Harry tapped on Jane's door and said that breakfast was ready.

123

Jane had it standing up. William was there and standing up as he ate already. Within ten minutes they were on the road. The journey down the valley, their only exit, because of the half light was negotiated very carefully, but by the time they reached the coast all the morning shadows had gone, and it was a shiny day full of sunny premonitions for a shiny afternoon.

They went down the south coast road, San Marco and Ruthven in open boxes so they could enjoy the morning as well. A soft explosion of little waves came up at them from the strings of yellow beaches beside the road, a musical scrabbling of surf-sifted pebbles. It was a beautiful ringing sort of day.

'I suppose we're mad,' laughed William Bower, in a ringing mood, too, Jane saw, 'apart from your exercising our two fellows are practically untrained.'

'They were trained at Little Down.'

'Untrained to our methods,' he explained. 'However, it will be experience, and, let's hope, a profitable one.'

It was. San Marco came in third in the race that Bower selected, and the newchum Ruthven actually shared a first.

'Now we can go down a grade,' said William on their way back, 'try a meeting with less of that English plush and lush.'

Jacumba, west this time, was selected, and here San Marco showed definite distaste for anything but green fields, but Ruthven frankly enjoyed himself, no place admittedly, but demonstrating a distinct lack of dismay over clumps of billy buttons and last year's thistle.

'The Downs now for Ruthven,' William decided. 'Agreed?'

There was no need for Jane to pretend to contemplate, she was as keen as Bower was.

'How long will that take?' she asked.

'Longer, of course. I'll have us flown, us comprising you, me, Ruthven, the previous day, then stay a day, then return the next day.'

'You won't pilot the plane yourself?'

'In a journey as far away as the Centre, no. I'll charter a larger craft, and just sit back.'

'Won't all that be expensive?'

'Thinking of your fifth, Miss Sidney?'

'I could be.'

'Then hope to recoup it all in the race that I have my eye on. Anyway, tallying up what the boys have already won you, you should break even, even if we lose.'

'That's all right,' Jane assured him, 'I'm well aware that in this business you have to take a risk.'

'. . . Only in this business?'

Something in his voice stopped Jane from answering him with a question of her own, a question as to what he meant by that question. Instead she asked when and where.

'Tuesday next. We'll leave early again and pick up the craft at Quinton.—By the way, Miss Sidney.'

'Yes, Mr. Bower?'

'These Centre meets are social as well as racing events. I'd pack something more than jodhpurs.'

She would have liked him to be more explicit, but he turned and went.

She asked Maureen that night. It was good to have something to ask the girl, Jane thought; the way things were now, Maureen growing progressively more and more withdrawn, apart from the feeding of the foal and the problems to be discussed, they never spoke with each other.

'Long dress,' Maureen said abruptly.

'I haven't brought one.'

'You can have mine. It's long and white.' Maureen's voice was more clipped than ever.

'That sounds like a wedding dress.'

'It was.'

'Maureen . . . Maureen dear . . .'

It was no use, the girl had left. When Jane went along to Maureen's room and tapped on the door, she was not answered.

They drove to Quinton the next morning, Ruthven looking regally pleased with himself riding along in a float intended for three. William Bower had taken the extra precaution of padding the box in case Ruthven in his solitary state bumped around over any rough patches, but he had still left Ruthven with a good viewing section. Jane was pleased about that; she had inherited from Rusty a firm belief in horses having an unrestricted view when they travelled.

They passed through the valley beneath eucalypts, black-woods and sassafras, waved to millmen milling big logs and piling pale hummocks of sawdust, called to the children from farms and hopfields hanging out mailbags for the mailman, then reached the coast with its soft burst of waves and washing pebbles again.

Quinton, much larger than the rural strips Jane had encountered so far, was not far distant. When they got to the field a moderate-sized freighter was awaiting them, with a crew of two, the second pilot doubling for a wireless navigator, a comfortable section for Ruthven and two easy seats for the passengers. The engines whirred, they taxied, rose above the coast and at once set off west.

They crossed the Divide, and for a while rural centres displayed their pattern of streets and parks fairly frequently, then the country cities disappeared, the flats flattened out even further, and salt pans, and clay pans, and eventually the desert took over. Jane stared down fascinated at red ochre sand, purple patches of Calamity Jane, or so William Bower told her, and outcrops of rocks taking on almost unbelievable colours.

'I only hope,' said William, 'that Ruthven is as impressed as you seem to be.'

'Oh,' breathed Jane, 'I really am.'

Several hours afterwards the engines changed their beat and Jane knew they must be ready to put down. She could see little to descend to, only a few scattered buildings, surrounded, as was everything here in the Centre it seemed, with endless space.

'Is this Farley Downs?'

'Yes. You mightn't think much of it commercially, but it's still the recognized hub for a thousand mile square. Also, it's the accepted social centre.' A slight laugh. 'Believe it or not, people will be attending this meet from even further than those thousand miles.'

'How do they get here?' she asked.

'By truck, jeep, 'rover, plane, whatever means they can rustle up. We won't be the only charter, either, you'll find a dozen of them flying in, some carrying as many as six horses. Then, of course, there'll be the sideshow men in caravans, the picture showman, Ahmed the Afghan, and the last, I think, of his breed in the west, with his covered waggon full of pretties.'

'What kind of pretties?'

'Dresses for milady. You didn't think,' William laughed, 'there were shops out here?'

'I thought there might be a vestibule in the hotel.' Jane was thinking of the very attractive shopping she had encountered in many hotels.

'No hotels here,' said William, 'only pubs.'

'Aren't they the same?'

'There is,' William Bower said cagily, 'a subtle difference, Miss Sidney. You'll see.'

'Are we booked into one?'

'There is only one. And no, we're not. Thank heaven.'

'But why? Then where are we to stop?'

'Why, because I, anyway, want some rest, and rest you can't expect when Centralians who haven't seen each other since last year meet up again. No, we're rooming at the Marriotts', old customers of mine. I sold them a winner two years ago, since when I'm an even more welcome guest. I say even more, for everyone is welcome in the west.'

When the plane put down, Jane could see why William Bower had been glad of the Marriotts. The landing paddock was practically in the town, if you could call one weathered timber hotel and one small post-office that, and already the town was humming.

'The hotel—pub has swinging doors!' delighted Jane.

'And a well-worn counter.' William watched her fascination at the ten-gallon hats with their owners underneath coming out of the dusty street with frothing glasses.

'You must try a beer,' he said, 'they have a very fine art of putting on big white collars to them here.' When she shook her head, he agreed, too, to wait.

'Until we celebrate our win,' he grinned.

They found a truck willing to take them out to the Marriott's.

'Ruthven?' Jane asked.

'Bob Marriott has a stable here in town and has agreed to put Ruthven with his fellows.'

It was not far out, William said, to the Marriotts'; they were lucky there, for most of the other entrants, unless they had secured a hotel room, which was unlikely as each room was pre-booked from the previous year, and even then never catered for less than seven or eight on beds, sofas, divans and what-have-you, would be up to a hundred miles away.

'And you think Plateau is isolated,' he finished.

'I've never said so.'

'No,' he agreed after some thought, 'you haven't. Actually, Miss Sidney, you don't say much at all.'

'Is it required?' she asked.

He pretended to be thinking. 'I can't recall it on the agreement,' he said at last.

The Marriotts had what William told Jane was a fairly typical Downs home. It was wide, one-storeyed, spread over what seemed an immense space, with green polished cement floors and coolness, a lot of bamboo and many bright rag mats. Mrs. Marriott, middle-aged and eager for female company, at once asked Jane about her dress for the hop.

'I should say the Race Ball,' she corrected, giggling.

'I haven't brought one.'

This caused Mrs. Marriott to cry out with disappointment and William Bower to say dourly: 'But I told you, Miss Sidney.'

'I know, but I hadn't one' ... for a moment Jane wondered what would have been the reaction if she had worn Maureen's wedding dress ... 'and there was nowhere in Plateau to buy anything.'

'Nor anywhere here,' said Mrs. Marriott. She added thoughtfully, 'Unless——'

'Unless I go in the afternoon dress that I did pack?'

'Oh no, dear, it has to be an occasion dress. A long one. You might find it hard to believe, but there won't be a woman at the dance who hasn't been planning her get-up all the year.' Her eyes met William's. 'I wonder——' she said.

'It's too late for David Jones, Marry,' discouraged William.

'But—— Ahmed?'

'Ahmed? Would he have anything for Miss Sidney?'

'It's not all bargain basement he carries, Bill, I've seen several things I wouldn't mind buying myself.'

'He's at the course, I expect.'

'Along with all the other itinerants.'

'We'll go now,' said William Bower, not asking Jane whether she wanted a new dress, for that matter whether she wanted to attend the ball.

There were plenty of cars at the Marriotts', belonging both to them and their staff, so getting back to Farley was no difficulty. Finding Ahmed proved more of a difficulty; already the outside of the ring was canvas city.

Jane looked around in fascination. Little Down had had its village fêtes, but never had she seen anything like this. There were trucks, jeeps, caravans, tents all huddled together, and beside them merry-go-rounds, hooplas and Aunt Sallys already snaring trade. There were balloon men. Pie pedlars. Hamburger Harrys. As a matter of fact there were five Hamburger Harrys, each Harry looking resentfully at the other.

'Tomorrow,' said William, 'you'll see signs Original Hamburger Harry.'

'On all of them?'

'Very probably. Here's Ahmed now.'

Ahmed had a covered waggon, and he had circled each side with his wares, mostly bright shifts and dangling baubles to wear with them.

At first Jane thought it was a waste of time, that there could be nothing here, then both she and William saw the long, fresh pink cotton number together, more simply made than the heavily beaded offerings beside it, in fact quite a possible dress, Jane had to admit.

'It's not Pierre Balmain,' said William.

'Nor, I expect, David Jones,' Jane smiled.

'Will it do?' he asked.

'So long as it doesn't offend you.'

'If it does, I'll only look the once,' he promised. He told the Afghan to wrap it up.

They did not come back into Farley that night, where, Mr. Marriott said, the swing doors would be swinging overtime. Instead they sat in the cool green room and talked Territorian. How interesting it all was, Jane thought, listening intently.

The next morning she put on the floral jersey she had brought and went into the big event. It was, she found, like nothing else on earth, it was completely, wildly, fascinatingly different, and she enjoyed every moment, even when William Bower said of her red ochre hair, for the stirred-up dust and covered that part of Jane as well as everywhere else, a laconic: 'I know now why my uncle signed you on as his strapper.' He nodded to her head. 'After a name like Rusty, how could he help it?'

'Rusty was short for Russell,' she reminded him.

'Yet probably a favourite colour with my uncle, too.'

'But I'm not red. Perhaps faintly inclined that way in a natural state, but still far from titian.'

'Who said such a nice thing of you as titian?'

·130

'So long as it's a removable colour that's all that concerns me,' Jane said plaintively.

'It'll come out in the wash,' William assured her. 'Have you seen around?'

'I've bought six lucky tickets and been unlucky six times, had a cornet of fairy floss, a——'

'Had tea?'

'Not yet.'

'Come on, then.' He put the tips of his fingers under her elbow and led her to the tent, where great urns of strong brew awaited, toppling piles of corned beef sandwiches, wide wedges of sultana cake.

Jane was intrigued with the jockeys, already parading up and down, not the professionals who had flown up from the cities for the main events, but the local offerings for the minor races, wearing everything on their heads from ten-gallon hats to crash helmets, and instead of breeches had put on shorts, chaps, jeans, even in one instance waist-high wading boots.

William told Jane that Ruthven was down for the Downs Cup, the main event. 'Ambitious of me ... of *us*,' he corrected that at once. 'You've no idea of the aristocrats he'll have to meet.'

'It'll be experience at least,' said Jane.

'That's all I'd bet on if I were you,' Bower advised.

He was entirely wrong, as he said proudly, if regretfully, an hour later.

'Had I known that Ruthven had that in him ...'

For Ruthven was first away from the barrier, led all the way, came in an indisputable leader.

'I reckon that boy was born for the mulga,' William glowed. He looked at Jane, then grinned. 'But someone else was not. You're Eve in ochre, Miss Sidney. If you want to wear that pink creation tonight you'd better tone down your colouring a little. Shall we leave now to give you time to soak?'

'The Marriotts are still here,' she pointed out.

131

'I reckon we can run to a hiring. In fact' ... serious now ... 'between us at the very minute we could buy the taxi. Do you know what that stake was?'

'No.'

'Then take a breath.' He told her, and it was so incredible she stared open-mouthed at him.

'That's true. Now you know why I wanted a spinifex sprinter, the prizes to say the least were rewarding. If you'll close your mouth long enough to rattle off some arithmetic, Miss Sidney, you'll see that your fifth entitles you to——'

'I'm rich,' Jane said unbelievingly. 'Not exactly, but you are comfortably placed.' He looked at her sharply. 'It could make all the difference, couldn't it? You could step out of the show right now. With the extra sum I'd pay you for your now valuable share you really could be that rich woman.'

'No, thank you.'

'Going for more?'

She hesitated. She had been going to say, as she had said before, 'I'll wait for the D's first, see them settled.' But all at once she knew it was not just that, that it was—— She fastened her teeth on her bottom lip to stop her making an audible sound of discovery, for she had just discovered an entirely mad, an entirely impossible, incredible thing. She had discovered—and she would not believe it—that when it came to this man, to this great, overbearing, overwhelming, over-*everything* hunk of——

'I should say you're going for more,' he drawled.

No, Jane knew, I won't. I won't.

As soon as she got to the homestead she soaked, scrubbed, shampooed. When at last she emerged, the tub wore a bright red rim, but Jane was her usual colour. Perhaps a little pinker from her long immersion, but it suited the rosy cotton. She regarded herself in the mirror and thought she looked rather nice.

The Marriotts arrived, dressed, too, then they all left in

the biggest of the cars for the Farley social event of the year.

Jane was impressed with the appearance of the barn, which had received much more attention than sweeping and dusting. The local ladies had adorned it in trailing ferns, native ti and flowering vines. With paper lanterns and balloons it became as festive a hall as any city offering, and Jane went approvingly in behind the Marriotts ... then stopped.

At the other end of the barn was a replica of her pink cotton. She dodged behind Bob Marriott so as not to embarrass the wearer just as a third pink cotton danced by.

'Well,' remarked William Bower by her side, 'Ahmed at no time said it was an exclusive model. Want me to drive you back?'

'To change into what?' Jane sighed.

Mrs. Marriott broke eagerly in: 'Ever since last night I've been thinking, Jane.'

'Good for you,' said her husband admiringly.

'Be quiet! I've been thinking, Jane. You see, I saw you in your negligée last night. So many girls now are wearing them for social events as well as home relaxation, or so my fashion mags tell me. You *could*, you know.'

'Well, one thing,' admitted Jane ruefully, 'I can't wear this.' For a fourth Ahmed creation had appeared. Followed by another pink. Then another. Ahmed must have won himself a considerable discount for accepting an entire batch of pinks.

'Come on, then,' William Bower said.

Back at the homestead, Jane took a long searching look at the garment. It was, as Mrs. Marriott had said, very possible. Also, she had done this sort of thing before back home. That buttercup brocade, she recalled, she had worn it to——

'What do you think?' she asked William Bower, holding up the article.

'Put it on,' he said.

Jane did. It was deep cream and it fell softly in a straight line to her ankles. It had a deep décolleté and no sleeves, but she felt it did not have a nightie look. She added shoes, beaded bag and went out to the room along the polished green floor, her heels making little clicks.

He was standing by the french window, looking out on the night, and surely no nights, thought Jane, were more beautiful than Centre nights, with their overdone stars and their big ... melon-big ... moons.

'Well?' she asked.

He turned around.

He looked at her. And looked. It took such a long time that Jane found herself squirming, found herself wanting to cry out not 'Well?' but 'WELL!'

Then, still looking, but what sort of look it was, amused, unamused, mutual, Jane did not know, for she found she could not look back to find out, he said: 'I think its original purpose is best, Miss Sidney.'

'You mean——' Now Jane did look at him, looked angrily at first, and then——

'Yes, I mean that,' William said in a quiet voice.

CHAPTER SEVEN

BACK once more at Plateau, Jane found herself less work-harassed than before. San Marco had been passed on to appropriate hands for specialist preparation for the better class provincials, and eventually, Jane suspected, a forth-coming Southern cup; Ruthven, having shown his rugged preferences, was being further toughened up at another of the Bower satellite studs—one, William Bower told Jane, dealt in similar conditions to the conditions, or lack of, that the Downs had provided. This left only Gretel, later to be mated, in Jane's hands, so Jane had only one girl and one orphaned foal to attend. She knew that her leisure period would be brief, in fact only till next week when the three D's emerged from quarantine, so she took the oppor-tunity, seeing she was not even required for the twins, Kate still eagerly retaining that position, to explore her new surroundings.

She did it on Gretel, and the pair of them enjoyed the runs across the flats, and, upon occasion, the cautious (for Gretel was a stranger like Jane was) descents of the easier sections of the cliffs.

Several times Tim called upon Jane for veterinary assist-ance, since Jane was at present the sole Bower member literally not run off her feet. It was that period of the year (Down Under version) when a stud, always busy, becomes near-hectic.

There were seven top-class stallions ready for siring, and every day floats arrived from far distances, some even from interstate. Records had to be kept, and to make it more time-consuming, at Bowers the hopeful mares were agisted free until after their pregnancy tests. It all made for more work again.

On top of this, the yearling sales were being arranged.

They would not occur for some time yet, but Jane appreciated from her Surrey days that they took a lot of planning, a lot of pre-determination and pre-selection ... and a few tears. Or it had been tears of goodbye for her. For dear old Rusty, too, she had often suspected. It was strange, Jane pondered, that however much you disciplined yourself on what had to be, you could not successfully discipline your heart. She recalled, and still felt a pang, Little Down's sadness over their parting with Village Square, Eastern Night and Darcy.

She wondered if William Bower, too, experienced tugs. She knew that he would have scoffed at the idea, even possibly repeated that 'pony high priestess' of his and Gair's, but she had caught him out several times on 'boys' and 'girls' and 'fellows', on observed unrehearsed looks, and she was not sure he was the strict business man he tried to appear.

He certainly wasn't when he sought Jane out one evening.

'A sale tomorrow,' he said abruptly.

'I hope you do well.'

'Thank you.' There was a tinge of impatience in his voice at her formal reply.

'Did you require my help, Mr. Bower?' Jane asked, still formal.

'Yes. You're not doing anything special, are you?'

'Only exercising Gretel. Maureen seems to be coping as far as Tim is concerned.' Jane said that a trifle tetchily; she had been a little put out at the vet's obvious satisfaction with Maureen.

William Bower nodded disinterestedly. 'It's Fair Honey,' he said. But this time with interest.

'Oh yes.'

'You know her?'

Jane nodded. 'A pretty golden girl with a——'

'Yes, with a nasty-looking scar on her hip. Up till now Fair Honey has discouraged buyers with that hip, as soon as

136

she goes into the sale ring and they see that scar they're frightened off.'

'How did the scar occur?'

'Honey cut the hip when she ran into a salt trough on a sheep property. It was before I got her.'

'Then you weren't frightened off.'

'I liked the girl at once. I mean the filly.'

Jane felt like adding: 'The mutual look?' but forbore. 'She's not that now, though, is she?' she said instead. 'Not a filly?'

'No. Fair Honey has had two very successful foalings. And that's what's concerning me.'

'Yes, Mr. Bower?'

'Because the catalogue hasn't been altered as I intended to alter it, Fair Honey is once more down for sale. Only this time her success as a mare could have leaked out, and there could be bids.'

'Can't she be withdrawn?'

'Too late. I've always made it a strict rule to stick to my programme.'

Jane nodded. 'Then what do you want me to do?'

'Bid, too,' he said.

'For myself or for you?'

'I wouldn't put you to that expense.'

'But if it wasn't such an expense?' Jane had had a thought.

He looked at her searchingly, but found nothing there. 'Just bid,' he advised.

'I still don't understand it; isn't the sale a yearling one?' Fair Honey was halfway now to two figures in age, Jane judged.

'The yearlings are months ahead. Even not being acclimatized yet you should know that. No, tomorrow's sales are just that. Sales,' he said gloomily.

'I'll bid,' Jane promised, taking pity on his gloom, remembering how she had felt on countless occasions. She added: 'If it's necessary.'

Again he gave her that curious look, found nothing once more, so left.

Jane went down to Fair Honey. She was an exceedingly pretty mare, and perhaps because of this received more attention than usual from the female strappers. Her coat was perfection, and Maureen ... or Kate? ... had worked on the scar until it was a very small flaw in the diamond.

But, said Jane to the mare, it's going to be a very discernible flaw, Honey.

It seemed strange to do things in reverse, to take the shine off instead of put it on, but that was what Jane worked at. She could not entirely diminish the gloss, as Honey was in excellent condition, but she did manage a discouraging lacklustre through untidy disarray to the shining gold coat. The scar showed out much more with the hair combed revealingly away from it. Jane even considered highlighting it by means of a cosmetic pencil, but she felt she could not cheat too much.

The next morning the country sounds of Bowers were punctuated in a way Jane recalled from Little Down. By raucous bid! By hammer! Always she had hated the blood sales, and she found she liked them no better now. But if the selling of Barbie, Mr. Six and Mahal upset her, barely knowing them, how much more upsetting must it be to William, who did? She would have liked to have flashed a sympathetic glance at him, but she was keeping an eye on Fair Honey, seeing that her scarred hip was in full view.

'And now, gentlemen, we offer Fair Honey, out of——'

Jane, taken by surprise, saw that she had not attended enough; she had let one of the grooms take Honey into the sale ring, and on her good side. She went to follow, but it was too late, the bidding actually had begun.

And such a beginning! It was a higher start even than Mahal had attracted, and everyone had had their eye on well-connected Mahal. Feeling a little sick, seeing her Farley Downs' profits vanishing for ever, for William Bower would never countenance this expense, Jane went higher.

The bidder—she could not see him—bid again. Jane bid.

All the attention was on her, standing as she did in the front row, and also, Jane knew from experience, because she was female, reasonably young, reasonably attractive.

Another bid from a retaliating Jane, and then, to her utter horror, even though it was doing what William Bower had asked of her, the acceptance from the auctioneer of that bid. An acceptance of three thousand five hundred dollars for a scarred mare.

Jane edged away from the ring and hurried towards the stables—just, as she had found years ago, as mothers find comfort in children, strappers find comfort in foals. She pushed the door of Wendy's Pride's box, and there, as well as Wendy's Pride, was William Bower. And he was laughing. Not just amused laughter but hilarious laughter.

'Your face!' he said, and laughed again.

'What's wrong with it?' Jane rubbed at her face with her handkerchief.

'Not now. Then. Then when you made that last bid and was accepted.'

'If you think it's funny——'

'I think it's side-splitting. Your poor worried little face!'

'It was a lot more money than I—than you intended,' Jane said unhappily. 'But what could I do? I did de-glamorize Honey.'

'The worst thing you could have done. If I'd known you had that in mind——'

'De-glamorization?'

'Is there such a word?' He laughed again. 'The moment I saw Fair Honey come in, saw her dusty coat, I knew all the wiseacres, and believe me most of them there today are that, would be wide-awake.'

'They were,' agreed Jane miserably, 'or at least one was. Does it matter much, Mr. Bower? Does it mean that you'll have to recompense your company for that very big bid I made?'

'No company,' William Bower informed her calmly, 'only yours truly in this concern ... except, of course, your fifth of the new lot.'

'Then?'

'No, it doesn't matter.' Again he laughed. 'Don't go fretting, Miss Sidney, all's well and all that, and it's brightened up what's usually a saddening affair.'

'Saying goodbye,' she nodded. She asked: 'Who was it bidding for Honey? Do you know him?'

'*You* don't know?'

'It was someone at the back.'

'And you didn't know?'

'Who was it, Mr. Bower?' For William Bower was moving out of the stable, yet not right out.

'Two thousand,' he called to show her. Then: 'Two thousand two hundred.'

Jane stared across at him. 'You,' she said.

'Yes.'

'But—but why?'

'The moment the mare came in I felt the interest, heard the stir, and no one reads a stir more clearly than a stud man. "What's this?" the atmosphere clearly said, "why is Bowers presenting a sale in an unpresentable manner? Watch it, it must be worthwhile." That' ... William gave a nod ... 'was what I received in the atmosphere.

'There were several very affluent buyers,' he resumed. 'You wouldn't know them, of course. I did. I decided the only way to put them off was to scotch the thing straight away.' Another bout of laughing. 'So, Miss Sidney, I did.'

'I was bidding against you!' Jane was not amused.

'Try to look at it this way,' Bower advised kindly, evidently taking pity on her, 'try to look at it as keeping out the big buyers.'

'All I can look at it is from the amused angle, the amusement, no doubt later, of all the stud.'

'Well, why not? It's not given to everyone to amuse.'

'You've made a fool of me, a clown!'

'A very nice clown,' he assured her. 'Also, it's not every clown can raise a laugh wearing his ordinary face.'

'Shall I paint it and get a bigger laugh?' she said bitterly.

'Just keep it its English pink and white, Miss Sidney,' William said.

'I——' began Jane, but it was all too much. Before a tear, which was fast welling over, fell on to Wendy's Pride's soft brow, she escaped. She heard his soft pursuing laugh, his assuring, 'Take it easy, no one will think twice about it,' as she shut the door behind her and went across to the big house.

At dinner that night she found out he was wrong with his assurance, though she had expected that, of course.

'Here comes Miss Moneybags,' greeted one of the boys.

'Can I put the fangs in for a loan, Miss Sidney? Something around two thou would do fine.'

'Beats me,' said Harry at the canteen door, 'how they didn't see it was the boss bidding, too.'

'He was right at the back and the attention, naturally' ... a flattering look which Jane in her present mood did not appreciate ... 'was on our girl.'

There was more delighted laughter, and Jane decided she might as well join in. After all, her purpose had been achieved. Fair Honey remained on at Bowers.

Only one person seemed unamused. Maureen did put on a smile so as not to be conspicuous, but there was no laughter there. It was because it entailed Jane, Jane knew. She knew also that she must have an understanding with Maureen.

The chance came when Maureen had to consult Jane concerning a new diet for the foal in her care, for Billy Boy had got beyond a mere bottle.

Jane had no doubt that Maureen had asked Tim first, and been referred to Jane, for there was a thinly-veiled reluctance in Maureen's voice as she told the senior strapper how Billy Boy was looking for something else.

Jane passed on her knowledge, knowledge learned in Little Down as well as Plateau. She advised Maureen to augment the new diet still with the daily bottle until Billy Boy wouldn't accept a bottle any more.

'You'll know when that time comes,' she smiled, and the absence of a smile on Maureen's face decided Jane that here and now was her time.

'Maureen.'

'Thank you. I'll see to that new diet at once.' The younger girl turned away.

'Maureen——' Jane repeated rather in defeat; how could you broach a subject to a back turned deliberately on you?

But—'Yes, Miss Sidney?' asked Maureen, and that 'Miss Sidney' did it. It gave Jane determination.

'You always called me Jane,' she said firmly.

'Yes, Miss Sidney?'

'Maureen, what's happened between us?'

'Was there anything?' Maureen had turned right back again. Her eyes and her face were hard. She had a pretty, gentle little face, and the change in her expression grieved Jane.

'Not strictly. I mean we weren't bosom pals, anything like that. For one thing, I was too old.'

Maureen said fairly, 'I've never thought of you in that way. I've thought of you the same as I think of Kate.'

'You're referring now to my age, of course.'

A pause, then Maureen said stonily: 'Of course.'

'If I've done anything to upset you, please believe it's been unintentional.'

Silence.

A little desperately, Jane went on: 'I'm referring now to that time when I flew back from Fetherfell with' ... a pause ... 'your fiancé.'

'He is not!'

'He was then.'

'I don't think he ever was. Not really. But please go on.'

'You don't mind me saying this?'

'No. In a way I think the thing should be cleared up, the same as you think.'

'Then I'll explain why I didn't come with Mr. Bower. There were two bereft foals, you see, instead of one.'

Maureen said impatiently, 'I know all that.'

'So,' persisted Jane, 'I came with Mr. Gair, and he ran out of fuel and we had to land in some valley.'

'I know all that, too.'

'Then,' said Jane a little helplessly, not knowing what else she could explain, 'you know everything.'

'Not quite. Oh, I know it's all over between Rodden and me ... that is if it ever was on. Sometimes ... most times ... I don't believe it was.'

'Maureen——'

'And the strange part is I can't feel unhappy over it.' The girl looked challengingly at Jane, challenging her to look back. Jane did, and saw that Maureen was telling the truth.

'Then, Maureen, why are you like this? We were friends, instinctive kind of friends. You came to me.'

'And you must have been laughing your head off!'

'I wasn't. I was trying to know what to say.'

'It should have been easy enough. Just four words.'

Jane looked up at Maureen.

'Four words concerning my ... *our* ... ring. Just "I wore that once."'

'Maureen——' How many futile times had she mumbled that, Jane thought in despair.

'I liked you, Jane. I liked you very much. I would never have gone to Kate, who's a dear but immature, but I did go to you. Rodden is over—I just told you. There's nothing there, and, as things have turned out' ... what things? Jane wondered a little stupidly, for she felt stupid with regret for a friendship lost ... 'I'm glad. But you were different. I looked up to you. I—came to you. Oh, Jane, you needn't have deceived me like that.'

'How could I have said "Yes, a lovely ring, Maureen, I should know, I chose it." How could I have warned you about Rodden? I mean, what happened between Rodden and me could have been entirely my own doing. I still don't know for sure, Maureen.'

'Well, you'll have plenty of time, because it's all over so far as I'm concerned.'

'It was over years ago with me. So why ... *why* must we perform post-mortems like this?'

'It was your deceit,' said Maureen stonily. 'I needed you. I never had an older sister. I can't remember my mother, nor any aunts. You were just what I wanted. But you let me show you my ... our ... ring, and you let me come to you for comfort.'

'Yes,' said Jane, 'and I'm sorry about that.'

A silence came between them. Jane had apologized. She could do no more. She knew that time alone would bring reason to Maureen, and that there was no use trying to force matters now.

'I'm glad, anyway,' she said inadequately, 'that we've aired the affair.'

Maureen looked away, possibly ashamed of herself, but wisely Jane did not pursue the matter.

'I'd try that diet on Billy Boy,' she told the younger strapper, 'it's working for Wendy's Pride.'

'Yes, I shall. Thank you.' Maureen left Jane.

It could have been much worse, Jane sensibly realized. Maureen could have made a scene. More important still she could have put down her end-of-the-affair with Rodden as Jane's fault, but it was no one's fault. Maureen had simply fallen *out* of love with him ... or had she only ever thought she had fallen in love? Recalling Maureen's frank eyes as she had said, 'And the strange thing is I can't feel unhappy over it,' Jane believed this could be true.

Very soothing for Maureen, she accepted, once the indignation of being deceived by Rodden's former fiancée wore off, but no solace for Jane.

144

Doing what she always had done in times of doubt, stress or simply needing comfort, had done in Little Down before Bowers, Jane went across to the stables to press her head against a silky shoulder, fondle a soft brow. It never failed. She decided to have a run out.

Gretel was the only offering, unless she borrowed one of Bower's boys or girls. However, the mare liked blowing cobwebs away as much as Jane did, though Gretel's were only stable cobwebs when she would have preferred a meadow ... I must say a paddock, Jane reminded herself ... and Jane's were much more involved.

Saddling up, sympathizing with Gretel's whicker of pleasure, the pair of them, a girl and mare, left the stud behind them for Plateau's inviting green flats.

Gretel, as usual enjoyed every moment. She had never been a pernickety mare, Jane thought appreciatively, she did not step with female fastidiousness as many mares did once away from familiar turf. Jane remembered riding her once around a chalk pit, imprudent, perhaps, but she had trusted Gretel not to tread on any crumbling edge. Not that there were edges on the flat ... not until you actually came to the edge. Jane glanced in that direction. She had taken Gretel down some of the more gradual cliff tracks and the pair of them had loved it. Well, why not again? She was in the mood for diversion and Gretel was dependable.

'All right, girl, we'll go exploring.' Jane turned the mare down a path that looked as negotiable as the ones she had explored before. She was careful about that, she had no intention of being reckless.

It proved a pretty way. It edged round outcrops of rocks and entanglements of trees. Some of the trees met each other high above them to form a green arch. Once horse and rider passed a little stream singing down the valley, and Jane found a scoop of water from which Gretel enjoyed a long drink. If she had practised what she had practised on her previous explorations, and that was to go so far but no further, nothing would have happened. She and Gretel would have returned refreshed—and minus a few cobwebs—to the stud.

But, about to retrace their way, something between the trees caught Jane's attention. It was well below them, so for caution's sake should have been resisted, but the huddle, or cluster, or closer settlement of something, Jane could not have said what, intrigued her so much she felt she could not climb up again until she found out what it was down there. Gretel's whicker of disapproval, too, should have put Jane off, for all horses have a tremendous sense of the unknown, but Jane chose to call Gretel lazy, and pulling on the rein she impelled the unwilling mare further along the track. Not, some minutes later, that you could call it a track any longer. Someone had been here, you could see that from the bent bushes, but it was not a path even in the faint way that the other paths had been, it was practically nothing.

Several times Jane lost even the bent bushes, but, peering between the trees, she could still glimpse the huddle. It was a kind of get-together of rough logs, she saw, probably a crude humpy, as she believed these bush shelters were called here. Yes ... peering closer ... it was a humpy, a shack, a shanty. It would be the place the twins had visited the day that John had taken her to the eucalyptus distillery and they had sauntered off. Well, she would do no visiting. She was about to turn the disapproving Gretel back to the track proper when she saw a figure coming out of the huddle, and, not wanting to be seen herself, she climbed down from Gretel.

She looked between the leaves of the trees. John had spoken of this occasional bush visitor as an old man, but this man definitely was not. Then Jane was recalling Roberta as saying also on that occasion: 'Not so old.' She wondered——

Deciding she had looked enough, Jane turned to see a fed-up Gretel disappearing through the bushes.

'You bad girl!' Jane gave pursuit.

She did not know how she lost sight of Gretel, one moment the mare was rounding a bend and the next moment, Jane having gained that bend, there was simply no mare there. Nor at the side. Nor behind her. Nor anywhere. Gretel it seemed had vanished into air.

Now Jane did what she knew, but temporarily forgot, a walker in a new territory must never do: she plunged into the bush without first marking herself by some bend of the track, some peculiarity of a tree. Within moments, within yards, from the path, she was lost.

She pushed through tanglewood to find a small stream running down the valley—the same rivulet she had met earlier, she wondered, where Gretel had found a scoop from which to drink?

Its waterbells tinkled louder further down the gorge, which meant it must hasten its pace to leap somewhere, probably it became quite precipitous, so Jane turned back. If she could climb a tree she might be able to pinpoint herself, even find that lean-to in the bush and make her way towards it, but all the trees around soared straight and sheer for many feet, and even then did not offer any accommodating branches until much nearer the top. They were essentially valley gums, and reaching up to the sun.

She walked on ... though stumbled would have been a better word. There was not the slightest semblance of any path now, in fact there was nothing at all but dark green undergrowth, sage green bush and trees, trees, trees.

She must not panic. That could be fatal, she knew, she could go around in circles, exhausting herself, confusing any rescuer ... if rescue came. She presumed that Gretel would find her way back as most horses did, but she was remembering, too, that Gretel was a new chum, as she was, and could take hours to do that. By then it would be dark, and any search would have to be delayed until the morning. The thought of spending the night in this unfamiliar bush dismayed Jane so much she forgot her determination to

147

think and act calmly, and began pushing through the tangle-wood again, this time with abandon.

A sharp scratch from some thorny bush pulled her up sternly. She took stock of herself. She was scratched, blistered, tired, and ... if she thought about it ... hungry. She had cut her knee, though she could not recall doing it, a twig had ripped her blouse, she had slightly but painfully turned an ankle. On top of everything she felt giddy, light-headed, unreal. Also she felt afraid.

She found a smaller rock outcrop and sat down. It was hard to force herself to do it, every impulse in her urged her on ... and out. But on, she knew now, was not necessarily out, not the way she had gone so far. She tried to think rationally, plan reasonably, look around her and assess and consider. But every stir in the bush set her nerves pounding, and when a lizard came over the rock in search of sun she gave a little scream, jumped to her feet and ran wildly forward again.

Undergrowth stopped her once more, so she came back, but not to the outcrop and the lizard, for all that, too, had gone. Only the baffling tanglewood remained. I'm lost, hopelessly lost, Jane knew, and unable to think even now, she gave way to helpless little sobs.

After that she stumbled on, stumbled back, walked entirely without plan or reason. She was crying openly and she let herself do it. If I exhaust all that, she thought, I might be able to make some sense at last.

It happened that way. Utterly depleted and exhausted, she began walking in a more restrained manner, looking where she went instead of stumbling blindly through her tears. And it was then she saw the humpy once more, the small huddle between the trees. She saw the man she had seen previously ... or had she? This man seemed younger, taller, or was her imagination playing tricks with her? She had no opportunity to check up again, for the man went back into the shelter.

It didn't matter, anyway, she simply had to get down to

that shack and tell her story. All her prior distaste at meeting the hermit, for only a hermit would live like this in the bush, had left her now. She needed human contact, then a direction home.

She hurried down, always keeping the little clearing in sight. Then at last she was on it, sliding the final steep slope to the crude lean-to of bushes, roof of several iron sheets, sapling walls.

'Is anyone there?' she called breathlessly, and heard a movement in the humpy.

The man came to the door and Jane stared in disbelief.

It was Rodden.

Afterwards Jane knew she must have lost contact for a few moments. She could recall pitching forward, being caught in Rodden's arms, but then nothing more until she opened her eyes and found herself in the tiny dark hut. Still in Rodden's arms.

'This time I could make something of it, couldn't I?' Rodden's lips twisted in a crooked grin.

'No!' Jane said it definitely for all her weakness, and the man nodded.

'I know, Janey.' He released her and got up. 'There's nothing there. But at least' ... ruefully ... 'you needn't have scotched me with Maureen.' He had left her now to go to a Primus stove to pump it and put on some water to heat. She saw him take out lint, adhesive tape, scissors, a needle that he proceeded to sterilize.

'Are you going to mend me?' she asked.

'Yes. You don't deserve it, but I am.'

'I didn't do anything against you as regards Maureen, Rodden, it was entirely her own decision. Anyway, wasn't that what you wanted?'

'Only if I couldn't have you, Jane, and perhaps had I known——'

'Known what?'

'Known *for sure* that Maureen was to inherit a penny or

149

two come the age of twenty-five, because it was being mooted around. But I didn't know.' (Evidently, thought Jane, he did not know of her own improved financial state.)

She said in disgust: 'Rodden, you're nasty!'

'I have to be nasty. I had the misfortune of landing poor parents. Oh, they educated me, and I won scholarships, but a man needs more of a boost than that. I want my own business, Jane, I don't want always to kow-tow to a boss.'

'Is that really why you renewed your friendship with me? Because of what Rusty gave me?'

'Partly,' he admitted, 'though still something persisted from that first time. I was a fool, Jane, I wanted the hand-out that Bower gives all his employees on marriage at Plateau, quite a considerable one; no doubt he likes to play the benevolent squire. When you've had nothing all your life things like that count.'

'They do to you. They counted, anyway, more than I did.'

'Not really, but I didn't realize that until it was too late. I was attracted by Maureen, she's a pretty little thing, and that inheritance rumour was being mooted around even then.

'Then you came. My real love plus a positive income, not one falling due reputedly at twenty-five.'

'Rodden,' said Jane again, 'you're quite impossible.'

'But at least I'm honest.' The kettle had boiled and he was pouring the water into a bowl, adding some salt. He worked efficiently, but then he was a qualified vet. He came across to Jane with the bowl, a towel, the rest of the equipment.

'I've got OUT from Bower. I suppose you knew that?'

'How would I?'

'I imagined you might be chummy.'

'We're not.'

'Well, I have to go. Some other underling post, no doubt.'

'You were boss at Fetherfell,' she pointed out.

150

'Still an underling post. I want my own place, Jane, and that's why . . .' He did not finish. Instead he got busy on her injuries, and his touch was professional, gentle yet firm and very thorough. He let out blisters, applied tape, bathed, dabbed, dried, pressed, soothed.

'You're a good doctor, Rodden,' she observed.

'But a rotten vet?'

'You're not.'

'No,' he said ruefully, 'I'm not.' He looked at Jane. 'How come you're here?'

She had been about to ask him that for herself, but she answered briefly, telling him how she and Gretel had explored a new track, and how she had seen the humpy through the trees and dismounted to look closer.

'A man came out, but he wasn't you.'

'You're having delusions,' Rodden said lightly. 'The bush does that.'

'Then it was?' She supposed that could be, the humpy had been some distance away.

'It was I, Jane dear, only don't give me away.'

'Give you away?' she echoed.

'To the big boss. I'd sooner remain incognito when it comes to my retreat.'

'This is your retreat?'

'Why not?'

Why not, Jane thought, everyone should have somewhere secret to go, only . . . and she frowned a little . . . a retreat did not seem like Rodden.

'I'll get you up to the top now, Janey, if you feel you can make it. I'd brew some tea, only by leaving at once you could catch up on your mount.' He said it rather hurriedly, and Jane had the idea he wanted her out as much as she wanted it.

'Yes, I can make it,' she nodded.

She did . . . with Rodden's help. He knew a short-cut to the top, steep but accessible. And there, actually only cropping a few yards away, Gretel waited. She would not have

151

waited after sundown, Jane knew, but the fact that she had waited at all sent Jane running forward to kiss the mare instead of scolding her, as she had intended, for running off.

'If you go at once you should escape any notice,' Rodden advised. 'When I came past there was general stud activity in the northern field, and that's the furthest away so the longest return to the house.' He paused. 'Don't forget, Jane.'

'The retreat?'

'Yes.'

'What do you do there, Rodden?'

'I could say paint, compose, write poetry,' he parried.

'You!' she said disbelievingly.

'Credit me with it, or not, at least keep it to yourself. I have patched you up, remember.'

'Yes, and thank you for that.'

'Thank you for everything, Jane.' He said it sincerely, or at least, Jane knew, with as much sincerity as he was capable of.

'Friends?' he asked as he helped her mount.

'Yes, Rodden.'

'And silence?' He nodded back to the valley.

'Yes, Rodden,' she promised hurriedly. She was anxious to get home before the others.

She did it, but barely. She bathed, did some more patching to herself, then saw to it at dinner, and afterwards, that she did not move around any more than was necessary, in case her injuries showed.

William Bower fortunately did not appear for the meal. She saw him only briefly afterwards, and in the more muted light of the hall.

'Good evening, Miss Sidney, you're looking pale. Was it the strain of the auction, do you think?'

Of course she was pale, she had put on a thicker make-up than she had ever worn before. She wondered if he saw that, if he saw the scratch that the powder was concealing.

—Or so she had hoped.

'I trust it passes over, whatever it is.' His tone was carefully casual. 'Because tomorrow it's on again.'

'An auction?'

'No, your collection of your second batch. You'll leave early as before. Take a few days.'

She was quiet. She was thinking of the numerous cuts and bruises as well as the facial scratch she had suffered, she might camouflage them from this man by night, but by day——

'I won't be going this time. Tim will accompany you.' He added: 'And Maureen.'

'For convention's sake,' she said flippantly ... also with relief, relief that she would not have Bower's sharp eyes on her tomorrow.

'Oh, I have no fears about *that*,' he reminded her, and she knew he was baiting her with that family unit episode. 'Five a.m., overnight bag, you know the drill,' he tossed. 'Also, can I advise less of what you have plastered on your face? It's a long trip and it can play the devil with a woman's make-up. And after all' ... a pause ... 'a scratch is still a scratch. Who did it, and why, Miss Sidney?'

'A bush, and because I ran into it,' she said in angry frustration. This man simply missed nothing at all!

'Well, it's you who's suffering,' he dismissed carelessly. 'Have fun.' Without another word, he went away.

She knew she had been let off lightly, if he had really wanted to know he would have persisted, and she might have had to tell him.

She went upstairs, tired after the day's happenings, inexplicably discouraged even though she had escaped quite well, all things considered.

Then she was realizing with a leap of her heart that she was collecting Dandy tomorrow. Dotsy and Devil May Care, too, but Dandy. Dandy.

Jane was smiling as she fell asleep.

CHAPTER EIGHT

TIM picked up the three D's quicker than William Bower had collected the first contingent. He spent less time on meals than the stud master had on Jane's first Sydney trip ... Jane recalled lunch and the long discussion on the value of Dandy, the condition of Dotsy ... which meant he could get the horses out of quarantine earlier, then have them ready for their journey home.

On the second day of the collection they followed the highway instead of the longer mountain road, and by dusk were back at Plateau. It had been a pleasant if uneventful journey. Several times Maureen had put out awkward feelers of friendship. If Tim had not been there, Jane would have said, 'Darling, it's all over, it was all the silliest thing, anyhow, but it's passed and now it is the past.'

As they crossed the little bridge they saw the twins racing each other over the creek. Kate was not with them, but with swimming efficiency like that they did not need her.

'Hop-picking festival next week,' Tim remarked. 'Ever been to one, Jane?'

'No.'

'It's something not to be missed, not here, anyway. Every nationality in the world, every tongue, every dance, every drink, every dish. It's a great show. John will want you to go.'

'I doubt it. I haven't seen him since *Kate* took over.' Jane emphasized Kate slyly.

'He'd be out of luck if he wanted to take Kate,' Tim laughed.

'Be quiet,' said Maureen sternly. She said evasively to Jane: 'We all go, it's tremendous fun.'

'It sounds it,' Jane nodded, wondering why Tim had been

silenced.

But Jane could not wonder about anything very much, she was too happy because of Dandy. Although the other pair had clearly recognized her, it had been Dandy who had greeted her. The tears had been streaming down Jane's cheeks as she had put her hands on each side of the satiny head and pressed her lips on the big brow.

She had had no time to consider Dotsy, whether what William Bower had said of her was right, or otherwise. However, she asked Tim on the way home, and he said he couldn't be sure, either.

'A vet?' she queried.

'That's right, Jane.'

'But you've been giving pregnancy tests to the mares who have been in for service.'

'Yes. We always do, for at that stage the tests are simple. But Dotsy, if she is, would be well on by now, and, strange though it seems, not so easy. For on the other hand she merely could be well on with plain avoirdupois ... as Gretel was. You have to take your time over an opinion at this stage.'

Jane questioned Dotsy herself that evening. Dotsy was a nutty brown, very glossy, and certainly showing a slight rotundity. But it needn't be pregnancy, as Tim had said, it might just be a tub, the same as with Gretel, that Dotsy had grown through idleness and overeating.

'Are you or aren't you, Dotsy?' Jane asked.

Dotsy whickered.

'Who was it?'

Dotsy, Jane could have sworn, winked.

'You're a shameless girl! I'll have to write to Rusty.'

'It's high time you did.' That was Jane's first indication that she had been talking aloud and that William Bower was standing at the door of Dotsy's box listening. 'I thought it had been written long ago, and that this was the answer.' He held up a letter with an American stamp.

Jane put down her working tools and came across to

155

claim it. About to slip it in her pocket for reading afterwards, she remembered that this man was Rusty's nephew,
so opened it instead.

There was nothing that couldn't be shared. Rusty loved
the part of America in which he found himself, he believed
he would be happy there until it was time for him, too, to
be put down.

He asked about the boys and girls, and, on second
thoughts it appeared, his nephew.

'Nice of him,' broke in William drily.

'Most of all, you, Jane.' Jane read that aloud before she
could check herself. 'Are you contented? Are you happy?
Have you exchanged any mutual look?' Jane stopped, annoyed with herself, annoyed with old Rusty.

'Go on,' said William.

'That's all,' she said.

'Well, have you?'

'Have I what? No' ... impatiently ... 'don't bother to
answer. It's all too silly. Anyway, it's no business of yours.'

'Agreed. But what is my business as your employer ...
oh, yes, I'm that as well as co-director ... is that scratch,
Miss Sidney. It's rather a deepish one. If you indicate the
bush that did it I'll have it cut back.'

'It's nothing,' she said evasively.

'It would have been something had it not been attended
to, I would say. Who did attend to it?'

'I did.'

'You did *later*, I think ... but I also think it was attended to fairly promptly, and by someone who knew their
job.'

'Like a doctor,' she said flippantly.

'Like a—vet.' He waited. 'So you met Gair,' he said
when Jane did not comment.

'I did not.' Well, actually there hadn't been a meeting.

'I happen to know Gair's particular manner of bandag-
ing ... good lord, I should, I've seen it often enough. That
ankle, for instance' ... his glance went down ... 'has been

156

bound in a different way from how a layman would bind
it.'

'I bound it myself this morning,' she insisted.

'Borrowing Gair's method?'

Jane was silent. She *had* borrowed it.

'All right, then,' Bower shrugged, 'it's not important,
you're not stepping on anyone's corns, Maureen isn't interested any more. You have an All Clear.'

'I don't want it.'

'Why not? Dead sea fruit?'

Jane was silent, furiously so.

'He's a clever fellow,' said Bower.

'Yet you're getting rid of him?'

'Let me finish, please. But not my kind of clever fellow.
He'll do much more and in a shorter time in a different sort
of place from Bowers.'

'He told me you'd sacked him.'

'When you met him?' he said deliberately.

'When we encountered,' she corrected coolly.

'Where was that?'

'Oh—somewhere along a track.'

'You surely know *where*,' William Bower said angrily.
'Good lord, if you didn't know you could have got lost.
Getting lost in our bush is very easy, but not easy on the
searchers. It's sometimes proved fatal for both sides.'

'I'm here, aren't I?' Jane wondered how his reaction
would have been had she confessed that she *had* been lost.

'So you can't indicate the spot?'

She could have told him the place where she had
emerged, but she had promised Rodden to keep his retreat a
secret, and she would not go back on that.

'Nor the track Gretel and I took,' she replied.

'What was Gair doing in the bush?'

'What I was, probably—exploring.'

'Not Rodden.' He looked at her sharply. 'Did you see
anyone else?'

'No.' For a moment she forgot that first figure that Rod-

157

den had laughed over when she had told him, had said was his, of course. 'Why should I?' she asked.

'No reason at all,' he agreed, but he seemed somehow uncertain.

He began talking about the new contingent. Devil May Care was going to start training at once. William Bower said he had been studying his records and believed they could expect a lot from him. Dotsy they must leave for Tim's verdict, or for when Miss Sidney got a reply from the letter she *still* had not written to Rusty.

'How about Dandy?' Jane asked.

'I can't see much of a sire in him, nor can I see a racer.'

'Does there have to be?'

'A stud isn't run for fun, Miss Sidney.'

'I know that now,' Jane said coldly.

'Keep the fellow for your own mount, I think we can run to that.'

'You're very magnanimous, Mr. Bower.'

He looked as though he was searching for a retort, but, unbelievable in William Bower, evidently he found none.

'Write that letter,' he directed, and went away.

'Dear Rusty,' Jane recited to her pretty brown girl, 'is Dotsy, or isn't she, for she won't say, and if so, when, and from whom?'

She wrote just that, that night.

Dandy and Jane had fine rides together. The pony was more venturesome than Gretel, and would have explored anywhere that Jane asked, but that last experience had given Jane an extra sense of caution, and, apart from a few woodsy rides along the upper valleys, the pair kept to the top, sometimes towing Wendy's Pride behind them, for the filly was out of her box now and testing her slender legs on the soft grass flats.

On one of Jane's rides, William Bower joined her. He rode a very large bay, Major, and beside Major, Dandy looked small and insignificant. Jane knew she must look the same.

'You like this, don't you?' They had come to the breath-less end of an exhilarating gallop. Jane, not towing Wendy's Pride today, had given Dandy his head. The pair had come first in the unofficial race. Perhaps, and probably, William had held Major back, but it was a nice feeling to win.

'I love it,' said Jane.

'I wish the twins were more enthusiastic. I've provided them with suitable mounts, but the interest just isn't there, only down the valley. It's discouraging to say the least, the Bowers always have had racing in their blood.'

'But they're not,' Jane reminded him tactfully. 'You must look to your own for that.'

'I have thought of it,' he said coolly.

The practicality of it irked Jane. She could not have said why she was so irritated; after all, it was no concern of hers whether this man married, or not, had a family, or not.

'You're disapproving,' he said, taking out his pipe, 'yet a union on that basis would possibly, even probably, make a much better union than the usual maudlin reasons.' He said the maudlin deliberately, she knew, to bait her.

'I've read,' he went on, 'that in spite of what people think, arranged marriages are much more successful than the eyes-meeting variety. Each partner knows what to expect, and doesn't ask for more than that. Do you agree?'

'I think,' said Jane, 'you have the right idea. For yourself.'

'Anyone else I should think of?' he asked.

'I also think,' she continued, 'that a grand tour of some of the studs might bring forth good material.'

'There's fair material here. I'm not the little boy who sees golden windows across the valley, I feel the talent is just as promising at home.'

'I thought stablehands were out?'

'A man can change.'

'Why not line up the candidates and see who wins the race?' Jane said, not far from open anger.

'It wouldn't be fair, unless I adopted a handicap.'

'Mr. Bower, this is all in bad taste.'

'I agree,' he said rather surprisingly, 'but you did carry it on, didn't you? I meant what I said about being regretful that the kids are not horse-minded. However, even if they were, it wouldn't matter, for they'll be leaving soon. I've had a letter from the parents. They've met up after their respective overseas assignments, and will be flying home within the fortnight.'

'The children will love that.'

'Yes, they will. Although lately I've thought...' But William Bower left it at that.

The next day invitations came up from the valley for the hop-picking celebrations, and immediately rosters were drawn up for attendance, since everyone wanted to go, and, on a stud, someone must always be on duty.

The girls consulted each other as to clothes. Because they were the fair sex, and the fair sex would be very much in demand at the celebrations, they were not rostered. Kate said that they must take an extra dress for the dance at night. Slacks, shorts or shifts would be all right for the day's entertainment, but long swinging skirts were called for after seven.

Jane, who had only her pink cotton bought from Ahmed ... and that negligée ... sent down to Sydney at once for some gay floral material. The girls did the same, and, their day's work finished, they met up in a bedroom for mutual sewing and advice. Maureen, as Jane had thought, was entirely out of her resentment by now, though still obviously a little embarrassed over herself and what she had said to Jane. One day they would shake hands and laugh over it all, Jane knew. Until then they both smiled a little shyly and a little uncertainly at each other, and the rift closed another inch.

Jane's dress featured large sunflowers, and, because she was slim and needed more bulk, she was advised by Maureen and Kate to gather the waist instead of adopting a

160

more slenderizing line. She was also persuaded to send for tangerine sandals and to wear a matching band in her hair.

'I'll look like an orange festival, not a hop variety,' she complained mildly.

'So long as you look festive,' they advised. They had chosen pink and blue respectively; Maureen would wear splashy roses, Kate spiky cornflowers.

Jane spoke to William regarding the children.

'They've enough clothes surely already. It seems to me I'm settling an account every week.'

'Not after-six clothes.'

'After six that pair will be in bed.'

'Oh, no, not when the hop festival's on. Roberta has been practising her steps for weeks, and I did hear Robert say he may join the Greek group, seeing it's strictly male. You can't expect them to do things like that in shorts and T-shirts.'

'I don't expect them to, I expect them to be put to bed.'

'By whom?' Jane ventured to ask. 'As far as I can see no one will be left here except Sam.' Sam was a pensioner-rouseabout, and not interested in festivals; quite definitely also, believed Jane, not interested in putting juveniles to bed.

'There'll be others rostered.'

Jane said nothing.

'Then I,' proceeded William Bower, 'am not incapable of putting a child to bed.'

'Two children.'

'Two children,' he said coldly.

There was a silence. Jane could see she would get no-where like this, and she knew how terribly keen the twins were to stop for the night's festivities.

'I would look after them,' she offered humbly.

'Between the reels, the flings, the jigs, the cariocas, the tangos and the rhumbas,' he came back disbelievingly, 'and that's only half the list. Every nationality down there, and, believe me, there'll be few nations left out, will insist on their dance, and with women-shortage as prevails everywhere here, you won't be off the floor to watch anyone.'

She could not argue that, not having been to such a function before. She stood uncertain a moment, then spontaneously she appealed: 'Please let them, William.' The moment she heard it, she could not believe it of herself. Not only the appeal to this man, but his *name*.

There was a silence. A long one.

'Very well then.' His voice was gruff. He did not look at her. 'Send down to David Jones for anything you need.' He walked away before she could thank him.

Robert wanted some mod gear. He made a list of it, and Jane, when ordering it, made the request that if it was not store-available, could someone get it for them from an In shop. Roberta simply wanted long skirts.

The clothes arrived, to both their satisfaction, and on Hop Day Jane packed their evening gear separate with her own, and sent them off ... they were going in a decorated haycart that one of the hands was entering in the procession ... in serviceable overalls.

She went in one of the jeeps, the rest of the unrostered staff in cars, bikes, vans, even horse-boxes. She noted that William Bower's car remained at his house, but then she had expected that, it would not be the sort of function, she thought, that a Big Boss would attend.

The barbecue and sporting events were to be held in the reserve at the creek, the hop-picking competition at one of the larger fields, and the dance on a floor that had been laid down on perhaps the only level ground of all the lower district. As Jane passed the setting for the night festivities, she saw that coloured lights were being strung between the trees.

It was impossible to believe that this busy, bustling place was their sleepy valley. The quiet, almost dreaming little community had burst into cheerful laughing life. The sound of the river that punctuated the gully silences, the songs of the birds, could not be heard for human noise.

There were tents and caravans everywhere, cars turned into beds, stretchers on tabletop lorries, sleeping bags and simply folded blankets.

The Bowers crowd went straight to the hop-picking, which, Jane was assured, was worth seeing. The picking was being done by families, and it was fiercely competitive. Each family was supplied a large timber-framed receptacle, and that was all the equipment needed besides nimble fingers. Jane appreciated the size of the receptacle, for it was as big as a horse trough, after she had tried hop-picking herself. She admitted ruefully that it would take a lot of leafy cones to reach one pound. Also, she was told, no leaves or stems were allowed.

The signal was given, and the families began to pick. It was really something to watch, Dad's large yet nimble fingers, Mum's, the children's, sometimes cousins' and aunts', all darting and dancing through the vine's thick leaves and sending continuous streams of little hops into the bin.

Jane did not wait for the winner, it would go on for hours, but she did do a tour of a kiln, its upper level spread with a ten-inch layer of hops under covering mesh, the drying floor on the lower level. The hot air was being drawn through now, and John, who had offered to show her, said, 'That steam should make you hungry. Feel like coming to the house for a bite?'

She had been looking at all the good things laid out for the pickers—chunks of sausage, slabs of cheese, pyramids of boiled eggs and tomatoes—and gave an eager yes.

'No Johnny cakes?' she asked, and John gave her a rather curious look.

'No. No, Jane. I thought ... well, I thought you knew.'

'Knew what?'

'Come and have a bite,' he said.

But it was not a bite, it was a feast. An exciting foreign feast redolent of olives, capsicum and spice.

'It's wonderful, John!' she exclaimed.

163

'It's Estonian. The same' . . . John smiled boyishly . . . 'as my girl.'

'Your——— But John, I didn't know. I knew that you were—well———'

'Anxious? I was. What's the good of a house without its woman? a home without its heart? Jane' . . . a little concerned . . . you don't mind?'

'*I* mind,' Jane leaned over and touched John's hand. 'I think it's great. What's her name?'

'I'll have her tell you herself, it's rather a mouthful, for us, anyway. She'll be back soon . . . her family are down for the picking . . . that's how I met her, Jane. She's lovely. I'm sure you'll think so. I call her Ennie.'

'And you're terribly happy, I can see that.'

'Terribly happy. And don't think it was as it must sound to you, I mean you knew I wanted to settle and settle soon. Well, it was like that, I suppose, but it was also a———'

'Mutual look?'

'Exactly, Jane. The very words.' He beamed on her.

But Jane could not entirely beam back. Then where did Kate come in, she was wondering, Kate who had been so anxious to keep on her valley commitments, Kate who had grown so much more mature lately, so much more attractive. Everyone had commented on it. She started to ask John, but his Ennie arrived, just as lovely as he had said, and after they had talked there was a Polish wrestling match to attend, a Latvian boxing bout and an afternoon singsong.

Then it was time to change for the night. Jane, Maureen and the twins changed at John's. When Jane asked about Kate, everyone was so intent on themselves she received no answer, but Kate must have changed somewhere, for later, half dusk now, and the lights by the dancing floor being switched on, she saw Kate in her cornflower skirts, and beside her a man Jane vaguely felt she had seen before . . . but where? There was no time to think about it, though, an Italian who had been strumming a serenade on a guitar nodded to several companions with fiddles, then drums came in, saxes, every instrument that could be carried along, the children even wrapping combs in paper, and the music began.

Oh, what music! As William Bower had told Jane, it went on the whole gamut. Jane was claimed at once and not let go through any national dance, even though she protested she did not know it. Even in the Greek dances, those strict prerogatives of males, Jane danced, as did all the girls ... Maureen with Tim, John with his Ennie, Kate with that man whom Jane had felt she had seen before.

A party of Spaniards down for the picking did the saraband and the fandango, the bolero was performed, some very spirited Polish steps, then an English group were showing quadrilles and Lancers, some Americans the old Cakewalk and the less old Charleston, and after that the foxtrots and one-steps were getting the crowd to their feet ... then the fiddles were becoming more muted, the guitars were picking sweeter notes, and the waltz was beginning.

Jane was in the arms of a young South American who had previously been showing her the intricacies of the tango, when the man cut in. It was such a definite cut there could be no protest. The handsome Argentinian stepped back ruefully as—— It was William Bower who calmly took over.

'You!' Jane murmured.

'Why not?'

'No reason, except——'

'Except you couldn't see me one-stepping and foxtrotting, Miss Sidney? You're right. But I think I can manage this one. Please complain to me if I can't.'

'I will,' she promised. Then: 'I didn't know you were here.'

'You know now.'

Yes, she knew. His arms were iron-hard around her, his fingers held hers lightly yet she knew the grasp was inescapable.

165

'You've been impolite,' she said for something to say. 'It's not a cutting-in evening.'

'It *was* not,' he corrected.

'Do you always ride roughshod over people?'

'I breed horses, I don't go in for the intricacies of riding them.'

'And other intricacies, Mr. Bower?'

'You're never explicit, are you, Miss Sidney? You deal in subtleties and innuendoes, never a spade's a spade.'

'Shall I now?' she asked demurely.

'Just now, little girl, you will shut that very pretty but tiresome mouth of yours. Have you no ear for music?'

She had, and for that very reason she had been chattering frantically, trying to escape the sweet gipsy strains that the strolling players were coaxing from their strings. For the penetrating beauty of the soft throbbing waltz was taking possession of Jane. She felt herself drawn closer and knew that he was taking possession, too. She knew by her instinctive response that she was not withdrawing from him. She half-closed her eyes, gave herself over to the tender music, to his light yet firm guidance, to the heady rapture of the swelling rhythm.

'Don't look now,' he said in her ear. 'We're the spotlight, Jane.'

He had never called her Jane, and for a while in her surprise she did not look. Then she realized that all the other couples had left the floor and that they alone danced as one person.

'Embarrassed?' he asked.

'No,' she said truthfully.

'I'm not, either. I think we're a team, Jane. I think...' William stopped at an arm on his shoulder. He looked thunderous. But it was not a cut, it was one of the Bower men. Chad Addison's face was grave. Jane tried rather hazily to recall which mare was due, or whether one of the horses ailed.

William went to the side of the floor with the man. The

spell broken, the other couples resumed dancing again. Presently the stud boss came to Jane and said: 'Addison tells me I'm wanted up top at once. I feel for all his insistence that it can't be urgent, because I checked everything before I came down. So wait for me, Jane.' Again he said Jane. This time: 'Wait for me, Jane.'

And Jane knew she would wait.

She did wait. She waited all that evening. As though they knew she was waiting, no one came after William went to ask her to dance.

After a long while she sat down to wait. She grew cold ... and as an hour, two hours went past, she grew indignant as well as chilled. How dared he treat her like this?

When she saw the dancers forming more intimate pairs, she knew she could stand it no longer. A group of the Bowers people were leaving on one of the lorries, so she went with them.

In her indignation she felt like seeking out William Bower, telling him what she thought of his conduct, but that could emphasize everything, suggest an importance that she might have put on the night's events, and she didn't want any importance conveyed to that man. Besides ... furiously ... there had been no importance, not to her. She repeated that to herself as she got down from the table-top and ran across to the big house.

He was coming out of it as she went to enter, and at once he flung out an arm and guided her away.

'I thought you'd never come,' he said hoarsely.

'I—I waited. You said to.' Her voice shook with resentment and she hated its betrayal.

'I know, I know.' He shrugged his shoulders as though to shrug all that away.

She could not understand him, he had been so different down there. Was he going on like this now to tell her that down there was not here, that the gipsy music and what it could have meant had stopped?

'It's the kids,' he said shortly.

'They're all right. Maureen and Tim are bringing them up.'

'I should have said their parents, adopted parents, foster-parents, whatever you like to call Gareth and Dorothy.'

'They're home?'

'They're not coming home, Jane, not this home—any earthly home. There's been a major plane disaster. Only a few survived. They were on that plane and their names are not among the survivors.'

He turned away.

CHAPTER NINE

WILLIAM had drawn Jane away from the big house, but they had not got as far as his house. A cloud had temporarily obliterated the moon, but Jane could still see the droop to his big shoulders, the tug to his long sensitive mouth.

'There could be some mistake,' she whispered.

'No,' he said. 'They were on that flight and the list is official.'

'The children.' She said that tremblingly, and he answered just one word.

'Yes.'

A silence encompassed them. It seemed to encompass Plateau as well. No leaf stirred, no night jay called.

'Poor little mutts,' the man said troublously at last, 'they've had more than their share, Jane.'

'Yes, William.' It came as instinctively, she knew, as his 'Jane' had come.

'Children are resilient,' she said presently, and he nodded back soberly.

'I know that, I know they'll recover. Thank heaven Gareth and Dorothy possessed the wisdom to tell them the truth. The question is how much did they know of it themselves?'

'Your cousin and his wife?'

'Yes.'

Jane looked at him in inquiry, and he went on, 'Did they know the real parents and the situation?'

'It's not usual,' Jane said.

'But, I think, in Gareth's and Dorothy's position very probable. I believe the twins came from their own circle, Jane. In time, being the wise people they were, I believe they intended to tell Robert and Roberta. But meanwhile they never got round to telling me, and now I don't know. I just don't know.'

'Do you have to know?' she asked gently. 'Can't you just accept them with love?'

'Of course. What do you think I am? But it's not as easy as that. Those kids are not a studman's children, they're a different breed. How can I make them happy when I don't understand?'

'They're children, William. *Children*.'

'Whose?' he asked. 'And how can they ever know now?'

'I think you're creating something.'

'I don't want to. I want to go and say to that pair: You're home. *Home*.—But they're not. I know it. They know it.' He looked at Jane. 'You do.'

'I don't, William. They like here. They're fond of you.'

'Fond,' he repeated hoarsely.

'Children are adopted every day,' Jane said. 'It happens smoothly, it's not the rough passage you anticipate.'

He listened to her, but his face remained crumpled.

'The thing is—I don't believe Gareth and Dorothy ever did adopt them. Oh, I know to all appearances they did, but I think they were really "keeping" them for someone, someone who might not have known, though Gareth and Dorothy did. Now—well, no one knows.'

'I really meant when I said that,' Jane came in, '*your* adoption of them.' She looked up at him.

'The studman takes a child?' he interpreted. 'Heaven knows I wish it was as simple as that. But it isn't, Jane. No, I was right when I told you I had to grow my own.'

'Love——' Jane endeavoured.

'Doesn't come into this. The kids like me, yes, but I don't *belong*, Jane. I'm an outdoor man, a factual character, anything but a person of finer perceptions, but I still know that, that I don't belong.'

'Then,' said Jane practically, 'the second-best will have to do, won't it? And children being resilient, it will do.'

'I suppose you're right. I suppose it's just the impact making me see a distortion like this. They'll recover. They'll settle down. Incidentally, in the shock I opened a

170

letter that was your—my uncle's. I'm sorry.' He handed the letter over.

Jane read it absently, her mind not on Rusty and what he had to say.

'You were right about Dotsy,' she said tonelessly to William. 'She is. Your uncle says when but not by whom.'

He nodded, and her heart went out to him because of the wretchedness in his face. She pushed the letter into her pocket.

'I'll write again and remind him, for you would want to know the sire. It makes a difference even before foaling if you're aware what you are about to handle.' She knew she was talking in the hope of diverting him.

He nodded dumbly again, William Bower, the self-assured studman without words! Gently Jane said: 'Do you want me there when you tell them?'

'Would you?'

'Of course.'

'Not tonight.'

'No,' she agreed.

'The morning?'

'Yes.'

In the distance there was the sound of returning cars, bikes, vans. In one of those vehicles would be two exhausted children.

They stood in silence as the revellers completed the run, drew up and tumbled out.

'It was fab, Father William!' Robert called.

'Jane looked the second-best of the ladies. Kate looked the best,' Roberta announced quite as a matter of course.

Then the pair both saw something together and called together: 'Look, two stars fell!' And watched them.

'Goodnight, darlings,' Jane said, and went back to the big house.

She awoke earlier than usual the next day, and put it down to the troubled sleep she had had. Then she heard the noise in the house, saw the glow at the window. She ran across and looked out. The glow was to the east, but it was not the glow of sunrise but fire. Jane knew that glow now after the fire at the hotel.

She pulled on her dressing gown and went down to the canteen. It seemed everyone was there, and giving their theory. It came from the valley, one said, and had been caused by a short in the lights. Someone else said that the night had been just a bit too merry and some camper hadn't properly extinguished his fire.

One thing, it didn't appear much to date, and once the Urara volunteer brigade got on the scene...

Jane went back, dressed and returned to swallow a cup of tea. She could not eat anything, she kept on thinking what lay ahead.

She crossed to the house, but no one answered her soft knock. Probably William was letting the twins sleep as long as they could. Probably he was too wretched still to come to the door.

Around ten, the glow that had been only just that, nothing more serious, considerably deepened. The news of the tragedy must have reached the staff, for as well as apprehensive about that spreading red-black cloud coming from the valley, the men were visibly shocked and quiet.

Jane set her shoulders and walked across again to the house. This time her knock was answered by Teresa. Teresa's eyes were red and when she saw Jane she whimpered. William must have heard, for he came down the hall, and if he had looked wretched yesterday, now he looked positively distraught.

'William——'

'They're gone,' he said flatly.

'Gone? You mean the twins?'

'Yes.'

'Then you told them?'

'No. They must have heard.'

'No one here would say.'

'Not intentionally. I'm not blaming Anders.'

172

'He told them?'

'No, but he's come to me and said that when his attention was drawn to the fire ... you know about that, of course?'

'Yes.'

'That he cried out: "Not that on top of the other!"'

'Well?'

'The twins were in earshot. They're not the usual kids, you know that.'

'Yes.'

'They must have checked. I can just see Robert doing that. He has his own transistor.'

'They knew their parents were coming?'

'They knew they were on that flight. I'd told them.'

'Perhaps they didn't check. Perhaps Anders only thought they heard.'

'I don't know,' William said wearily, 'I only know I've looked everywhere, and they're not here. Jane, what am I to do?'

How had she ever thought him self-sufficient, not merely self-sufficient but repelling even the smallest gesture of help? He wasn't now, for all his maturity, and Jane knew she had never known a more mature person than William Bower, he was still a little boy crying for help.

'Help me, Jane,' he said.

'When did you discover they'd gone?'

'The entire night I'd been thrashing over the thing. I came at last to the conclusion that I must tell them, tell them alone, that it wasn't fair to call on you.'

'That's not so,' Jane said quietly.

'After I reached that decision I must have slept at last. Anyway' ... a resigned movement of his hands ... 'I didn't hear the twins get up, go out of the house.'

'They must have crossed to the stables.'

'They did. Several of the hands saw them. Then later Anders must have remembered saying what he did. Being the pair they are, they would be consumed with curiosity. Hearing Anders say: "Not that on top of the other!"

173

would determine them to know what he meant. They would have come back to the house, listened to the radio, and——' Again that gesture of the big strong hands.

'But why would they go away?'

'I don't know. I was hoping you could tell me that.'

'William' ... how instinctively William came now ... 'how could I know? Ever since Kate has taken over I've barely seen them. They liked Kate, so I didn't intrude.' As she said it Jane remembered Roberta calling: 'Jane looked the second-best. Kate looked the best.' She recalled experiencing a slight pang of resentment, just a very small tinge, but there was no resentment now, only a great hope.

'Kate,' Jane said to William.

'Oh, yes,' he replied, 'I thought of that, too. But she's not here.'

'Then the twins could be with her.'

'No, Jane, Kate never returned last night. It appears she wasn't expected, she's on vacation. I didn't know, but then I wouldn't be expected to know. I leave these things to the bookkeeper.'

'Maureen could know where she's gone.'

'She doesn't. I've asked her. Though——'

'Yes, William?'

'I feel she might know something ... just a feeling. However, all I want to know is what's concerning me. The kids.'

'Have they taken any ponies?'

'No. You know how they are in that section.'

'But if they wanted to get somewhere——'

'They're also very good on their own two feet.'

'But not too far,' Jane said. 'They're only young children.'

'And already they've been gone three hours. It could be more. Jane, can't you think?'

Jane said wretchedly, 'I'm trying ... trying, but nothing comes.'

She left William and came back to the canteen and had a meal. She knew it was no use trying to think, to do anything at all on an empty stomach, and she had not eaten at all this morning. She knew if something did occur to her, and she went off, at least she would go replenished. She could tell by the look on Harry's face that he was glad to have a customer.

'Terrible food wastage today,' he sighed, 'breakfast hardly touched.'

'That cloud is getting bigger and darker, Harry. What will happen?'

'If the volunteer brigade can't handle it, it'll be all hands to the job.'

'Plateau, too?'

'Of course.'

'Has fire happened before?'

'Oh yes.' Harry seemed surprised at Jane's question.

'The valley looks so green,' Jane explained her remark.

'Eucalypts thrive on fires, they look dead, then the next spring they branch out bigger and better than ever. The ground section of the fires clear the undergrowth and the sun gets in and stimulates the sap, I expect.'

'How will Plateau know if help is needed?'

'There's a siren system been fixed up,' Harry said. 'I'm getting ready anyway, just in case.' He pointed to piles of sandwiches he was preparing. 'Have to keep the fighters well stoked,' he said.

The rest of the morning went leadenly. Although time was what they all needed, it seemed to Jane that the hand of her watch never moved. She tended Wendy's Pride, looked in on Dotsy, then went and saddled Dandy.

No one called out a warning to her as she cantered from the stable, they were all wrapped up in their own concerns, everyone was depending on everyone else to use caution and common sense. Jane would have used these, too; when she left the stud she had no intention of doing what she eventually did. But after she saw Maureen in the distance and crossed the eastern paddock to talk to her, caution and common sense did not come into it any more. Only a sudden, desperate feeling that the twins could be——

The words that Maureen and Jane had had together were back in the past now. Maureen met Jane with the same anxious look that Jane wore.

'It's frightful, Jane!'

'Can you help in any way, Maureen?'

'You mean as regards Kate, and where she is, and if the twins could be with her? No. I told Mr. Bower so. Definitely Robert and Roberta would not be with Kate.'

'But you couldn't be absolutely definite, you couldn't know for certain, could you?'

'Yes. Definite. Certain. You see——'

'Yes, Maureen?'

Maureen looked upset. 'I can't tell you,' she confided. 'It's not for me to tell.'

'Tell what?'

'About Kate. Anyway, she's on vacation, and she doesn't have to say where.'

'Do you know where?'

'Not exactly.'

'But fairly exactly.' Jane knew that was absurd, but she knew that Maureen would know what she meant.

'Somewhere on the coast.' Maureen sighed. 'She ... Roger ... well, I think they're being married.'

'You mean John and Kate.'

'No, Jane, you must have seen John and Ennie. It's Roger.'

'Who is Roger?' asked Jane.

'I don't know. I should, and poor Kate has tried to confide in me, but—well, I've had my own things on my mind.'

'Of course,' Jane hurried to reassure her. 'Then you would say the children are definitely not with Kate.'

'No. Not at her marriage. Oh dear, I wonder if I've said too much. Kate did ask me to keep it to myself. That's why I didn't tell Mr. Bower.'

'You haven't said too much, Maureen. Anything ... anything at all in a situation like this could be a help. Though what help this can be . . .' Jane bit her lip.

As she rode away again, she decided to report it all to William. It had no connection, but at least it explained Kate.

When she got to the house, William was not there. Teresa was still crying, so Jane came away and mounted Dandy again. She rode across the flats, taking several detours to look down to the valley. The pall of smoke had blackened and thickened. A wind was blowing up, and she watched it tear at the solid dark smudge, eventually severing it into two masses. Between and beneath them she saw a charred wilderness, and it horrified her. She had never known that fire could move so cruelly and so quickly.

In the canteen this morning she had heard men talk of wallabies caught in fire corners, of birds dropping out of the sky from heat when the flames leapt up. Flames were leaping up now. The wind, Jane saw, was changing again. All at once the billows of smoke had turned their direction, and red streaks of fire were whipping through the black. Even up here you can hear the roar. Down there it would be like thunder.

She watched until her eyes, red even this far away from the smoke, could not focus any more. She thought of all the people who had been down there yesterday. Thank heaven for the creek. Also for past experience, for she had been told, too, that no human loss of life was anticipated, not in a place that had had all this before, that knew explicitly what steps to take.

She went back to Dandy, a Dandy as usual unconcerned and contentedly cropping. They resumed their way until something that Maureen had said hit Jane. That was the only way she could have described it. It was like a blow at her thoughts.

Maureen had said: 'No, Jane. You must have seen John with Ennie. It's Roger.'

Roger? Who was Roger? Then Jane was recalling that as well as seeing John with Ennie, she had seen Kate with a

177

man. A man ... and her grasp tightened on the rein ... whom somehow she had felt she had seen before. But how? Where?

They had come to the section where the small track left the flat to go down to that part of the valley that Jane had explored on Gretel. Just here, Jane saw, you would not have known there was a fire; the wind, and therefore any tattered flames, had missed this section.

She pulled on Dandy and looked down. You could not see Rodden's retreat from here, but that, of course, had been Rodden's purpose.

Jane remembered that day when she had discovered it, remembered seeing the humpy between the trees. At the time Rodden had been the last owner of a retreat she could have dreamed up, she half-smiled.

Then the smile was fading. She was recalling that *first* figure, that figure that had *not* been Rodden's. Rodden had laughed at her, had said it was, but it hadn't been. She knew it now. The shack might belong to Rodden, though she doubted that, too, and undoubtedly it had been Rodden who had faced her there, who had taken her up the cliff again, but it had not been Rodden on that first glance. It had been——

Yes, it had.

Jane thought of Kate, Kate looking older, maturer, looking a woman at last, as she had walked beside that man yesterday, a man Jane had felt mildly curious about. She had felt she had seen him before, and now she knew where. It had been down there, down in the humpy between the trees. He had been the figure before Rodden.

Kate had been so different lately, Jane's mind ran on, so—so lit up. Jane knew Kate had liked her role of looking after the children, but had there been another attraction? A glow like Kate had worn had indicated more than the twins, it had indicated—— Indicated a man?

She was still asking herself questions as Dandy, obeying her touch, left the flat and began to descend.

The way seemed quite clear now. Strange how on a second journey you wondered how you had lost yourself the first time. Even when the track petered out, Jane still found a minor but clear path between bent bushes, by the pushed-back branches of trees, things that had not helped her before.

There was no sign of fire. As she had marked carefully on top, the wind had ignored this section. When eventually Jane did glimpse the humpy between the trees it was just as she first had glimpsed it. A cool retreat.

She had had to leave Gretel, she recalled, but Dandy just proceeded as though it was any ordinary bridle track. He stepped over fallen logs. He stooped and scraped under impeding trees. He showed none of Gretel's disapproval. The last steep decline he took sidewise, and finally delivered Jane at the bottom of it just as though she had been doing a leisurely round of the stables. She patted him lovingly, noticing, as she had several times this morning, a rather clammy sweat on him. She said: 'Dandy, you're not in such good trim as I thought—you and I will have to look into that.' Then, leaving him untethered, as she always did, since Dandy was no Gretel and would never leave unless told, she went across to the humpy.

'Is anyone there?' she called. 'Are you there, Rodden? Roger?' As an afterthought, she added: 'Kate?'

There was movement in the shack. The door opened. The sight she had longed for, yet not dared expect, met her eager eyes—the twins, red-eyed themselves. Robert and Roberta.

'Oh, darlings!' Jane called, and ran to the pair.

They stayed in her arms for a long while. No one spoke. They did not cry, Jane could see by their stained cheeks that their tears had been exhausted. She looked round to check if Dandy was all right and saw he was, then pushed the children gently back into the little hut.

'Why are you here?' she asked.

They had no answer for that; it wasn't that they didn't

179

want to tell her, thought Jane, it was simply that they didn't quite know themselves. And yet they must have had something in mind when they had fled here.

'They're never coming home.' It was Robert in a low but controlled voice.

'No, darling,' Jane agreed.

'Everyone was kind to us,' said Roberta, 'sort of special kind, so then we wondered.'

'We'd heard about a crash on our transistor.' Robert took up the story. 'We knew Gareth and Dorothy had left, so when people kept on being kind, we checked, and——' His little face crumpled, but he still kept back the tears.

'You wanted to be away from everybody,' nodded Jane. 'But why hide yourself here?' she asked again. She did not expect an answer . . . or the answer, anyway, that she got.

'To tell Roger,' the twins said.

'Who's Roger?'

'This is his place. He sculps here.'

'It should be sculpts,' said the other twin.

'You remember, Jane,' tacked on Roberta, 'the first time we went to John's and he showed us the stillery.'

'The distillery. Yes.'

'We got tired of it and came up here instead.'

'That was to an old man whom John knew, an old man who came down each year.'

'I told you,' reminded Roberta, 'that this man wasn't so old.'

'That old one never came this time,' Robert added.

'But why did you come now? You've worried us, children. We wanted to comfort you.'

They said, together again: 'We had to tell Roger.'

'*Why*, darlings?'

But they didn't know.

Jane didn't persist; they had had enough already. 'More than their share,' William had sighed.

'There's a bad fire,' she told them, 'and that's why we were especially worried. Everyone is out looking for you.'

'Not Kate,' said Roberta, brightening a little.

'She's being married to Roger,' said Robert.

'We knew Roger wouldn't be here, but we thought he might bring Kate back after the wedding. They call it a honeymoon then.'

'And you wanted to tell Roger?'

'And Kate.'

Roberta said, 'We're a bite hungry, Jane. You haven't any chocolate or anything?'

'We'll go up at once. Dandy is here and can carry you two. I'll keep close behind.'

They went immediately, and Dandy, cropping outside, came across almost as though he had overheard the conversation and had only been waiting for them. He stood docile as Jane lifted first Roberta, then Robert, up. She patted Dandy and they started off.

Afterwards Jane was to wonder agonizingly whether, if she hadn't put the two of them on Dandy, if—— But then if she had kept them by her, with her, could any of them have made it?

They did not reach the path before it came rushing at them, the wall of fire. This time the wind must have done a complete turn around, for previously the flames had licked only at the other side of the valley.

Jane looked behind her, the fire was spreading there, too. The only escape was up, and she slapped Dandy smartly and called: 'Up, up, take them up, boy!'

Dandy, now streaming with sweat, his soft brown eyes growing red as he blinked from the acrid smoke, obeyed at once, but Jane could see it would be an effort, the twins were solid children, and the incline almost precipitous. She ran behind Dandy, urging him, encouraging him, pleading with him. The fire still came.

Only that the tree fell between them, she would still have run with Dandy, though how, her breath coming now in gasps, she did not know, but the great trunk divided them, and in the roar of its descent, its flurry of leaves, Dandy could not tell that no longer was he being impelled up, and that was good, Jane knew helplessly, for Dandy would never have left her. He would have come back.

As it was, she saw him joining the track, racing up the track, the children hanging on.

'Thank heaven!' Jane said, saw another wall of flame coming towards her, and raced back to the shack.

She did not know whether it was a wise move or not, but at least the shack stood in a clearing, it was mostly iron, and there was a tank. She searched around for cloths of any sort, and soaked them in water. She splashed water around with her hands, for there was no can, no hose, as far as she could reach. She soaked herself. She did it until smoke overcame her, then she lay down. She remembered reading once that air circulated more freely on the ground.

She must have passed out, for she did not remember anything else. The first she knew was someone lifting her up. The air was still smoky, but she could see no flames.

'William,' she said to the face above hers.

'Yes, Jane.'

'Did Dandy fetch you?'

'... In a way.'

'Did he get the children up safely?'

'Yes.'

'Then bring you down here?'

A pause. 'I reckoned he'd done enough, girl, so I did the rest myself.'

'But he made it all right?' There was pride in Jane's voice.

'He made it,' William said, and there was pride in his, too. 'Now be quiet a while, Jane. There's a gang on the way with a stretcher. We'll soon have you in bed.'

'I'm not hurt,' she insisted.

'No, just smoke-filled, wrenched, scratched, sprained and what-have-you.'

'Is there anyone really hurt?'

'No.'

182

'Any*thing*?'

'Just relax, Jane.'

'Any——' The gang and the stretcher were approaching them.

'Just to make it easier for the boys, Jane, Tim's going to—well, after all, it's a steep haul.' Apologetically William stepped aside and Tim stepped forward and inserted a needle expertly into Jane's upper arm.

She knew no more until she wakened in a bed she did not know.

'You're in my house.' William Bower was sitting beside her. 'I thought it would be quieter.'

'But there's nothing wrong with me.'

'No,' William Bower agreed, 'nothing that won't mend.'

'There's nothing wrong with anybody,' Jane recalled from him.

'True.'

'Nor anything.' But he hadn't said that, she remembered. Her brain, still fuzzy, still uncertain, at least registered that fact.

'William.' She struggled up to a sitting position.

'Lie back, Jane.'

'You said—you said relax.'

'Then do it.'

'You said "Relax" when I asked you before.'

'Then don't ask now, girl.'

She looked at him ... and read him. Read what he didn't want to say.

'It's Dandy, isn't it?'

'Yes.'

'He didn't get up. Then how are the twins all right?'

'He got up. They're all right. But then——'

'Then you found he was injured? You found he was burned?'

'No,' William said quietly, 'then he died, Jane.'

He reached out his big hands to hers.

CHAPTER TEN

IT was a severance. It was almost like an amputation. Right from his shaky beginnings Dandy had been Jane's fellow.

'Cry,' encouraged William, and Jane did.

'Why?' she asked at last.

'He had a weak heart, Jane, it's as answerable as that. Dandy climbed to the top, then that was it. Fortunately a party of us were scouting around there at the time and saw Dandy coming up with the kids.'

'You say Dandy had a weak heart,' echoed Jane. She was remembering Dandy's clamminess today, remembering telling Dandy she would look into it. Only she had never guessed . . .

'Yes. Tim had suspected it and tested him. He had reported it to me.'

'Then why didn't you . . . I wouldn't have ridden him.'

'*That* was why,' William said simply.

After a while he went on, 'He was going to go, anyhow, Jane, how much better then with turf under his hoof and wind through his mane.'

'I can't understand Rusty,' Jane cried next.

'Not telling you? Or for sending him? The first would have deprived you of each other, you would have kept him in his box, cosseted him, and that would have been an earlier putting down for Dandy, a putting down in a manner for you. As for sending him . . . what else would Rusty have done?'

'Yes,' Jane said slowly, for Rusty would never have abandoned Dandy to someone else, and he never would have had him destroyed.

'It seems so purposeless for Dandy,' she fretted uselessly.

'With two kids' lives on his honour roll? Oh, no, girl.'

Jane was silent as she thought of that.

'We've both a few things to say.' William began again.

'Why did you go there, Jane? To the valley? Had you been before?'

'Yes.'

'And not told me?'

'I suppose I could say you hadn't asked.'

'Yes, you could,' he nodded. 'We'd never reached the confiding stage.' He paused. 'Then.'

She looked up at him, but he left it at that.

'You better tell me,' he said. 'I intend to know.'

'I went exploring on Gretel . . . you might remember you commented that day on my several cuts and bruises.'

'I do remember. They'd been professionally attended to.'

'By a vet.'

'You received a shot a few hours ago also by a vet. Tim. But I don't think it was Tim then.'

'It was Rodden. I didn't lie to you, I told you we'd met.'

'By design?'

'I went down to see the hut, and Rodden came out.'

'What was he doing there?'

'It was his retreat.'

'Oh, come off it, Jane, does Rodden look like that? Like a pilgrim to a poetic retreat?'

'No,' she said slowly, 'and I know now that it wasn't his place, then how was he there?'

'It's my turn for a while. I'll try to be brief. Gair had gone down to claim his pickings.'

'What do you mean?'

'My ex-vet had met Roger Reynolds in some pub and the usual talk had evolved. Reynolds had put feelers out concerning friends he once had, a Mr. and Mrs. Courtney, cousins, he believed, of the Bower Gair worked for. In a carefully offhand way, but not carefully offhand enough for our shrewd Rodden, Reynolds mentioned children.'

'Whatever for?'

'You haven't guessed?'

'No.'

'I'll tell you now, then. It hasn't been substantiated per-

185

sonally, but when Roger and Kate return I believe it will.'

'The children said those two were being married.'

'Yes.'

'I never thought ... I never guessed ...'

William lit his pipe, and they both waited for the smoke to wreathe up.

'Rodden saw Reynolds' deep interest and reached a conclusion. He told Roger he knew somewhere he could stay if he wanted to delve further.'

'It wasn't Rodden's place, then?' asked Jane.

'No one's place particularly, though John Rivers did say some old man came now and then. Reynolds rushed it, made up some kind of art reason he knew Rodden would accept, a reward being Gair's real and only concern, and Roger undoubtedly guessing that.' A pause. 'I'm sorry, Jane.'

'It's all right,' Jane said.

'So Roger took up residence,' William shrugged.

'How did he meet up with the children?'

'Through you, actually, in the beginning.'

'Yes, they wandered away from the eucalyptus distillery.'

'Later,' said William, 'through Kate. She followed them, being a responsible young woman, and then——' He smiled.

'I didn't know,' Jane said again. 'I could see that Kate had changed, matured, that there was a look to her.'

'A mutual look,' William said.

'But I still don't understand about this man and the children,' Jane continued.

'Do you recall that I told you I believed Gareth and Dorothy knew the real parents? That I suspected they were from the same circle?'

'That man is a sculptor,' Jane said quietly, remembering the twins' chatter.

'He was a very young member of that art circle, and because of his youth we must forgive him.' William tapped at his pipe.

186

'Forgive?'

'Forgive him for not waiting to find if a natural conclusion had brought a natural yield.'

'You mean——' Jane asked.

'Yes,' said William.

'Roger didn't wait,' he went on presently, 'he didn't even think. Not then. He had won himself an American scholarship, and he just left Lilith.'

'She was the girl?'

William nodded.

'Where is she?' Jane asked.

'She died. She was delicate, evidently. According to Dorothy's letter ... oh yes, there was a letter left for me by my cousin and his wife *in case*, but I didn't know that when I spoke to you before, I believed it was only a monetary direction.'

'According to the letter——' prompted Jane.

'Lilith was a leaf in the wind. Gareth and Dorothy were both artistic; they spoke that way.' William half-sighed. 'A leaf that would fall, were the actual words, and the leaf that was Lilith did fall, but the twins were born fine and sturdy, and they were adopted by my cousins.'

'Then Roger Reynolds returned?'

'Years after, and to a new circle. There must have been something nagging in him, for he asked questions, but no one had the answers. Then he remembered that Gareth and Dorothy Courtney had been closest to Lilith, a Lilith he had learned had since died. Then hearing in the way one does hear things that there were two children now with the Courtneys and of a certain age, he tracked Gareth and Dorothy down here just in time to miss them to ask them outright. Then he met up with Gair.'

'How do you know all this?'

'I told you, I have the letter.'

'Not your cousins' part of it, William, Roger's.'

'I spoke to Roger Reynolds an hour ago. He was just leaving for the church.'

187

Jane said: 'He will not have our children!' She said it hotly, unaware of herself.

But William was aware.

'They are not, Jane, and never were.'

'I love them.'

'I'm not exactly antagonistic myself. But they were not for me. When they learned of the tragedy, was it to me they turned? No, they went instinctively to Roger, and you know why, don't you? It was the call of the same blood. They're Roger Reynolds' kids ... and Kate's, too, now. I don't know if you noticed, Jane, but' ... whimsically ... 'Kate wore the best dress.'

'I noticed,' Jane said.

'A lot of water has gone under the bridge that Roger stands on. He's a mature man now. He can't be penalized for youth, Jane. Also, he wants them, and they, though they don't realize or understand it, want him.'

'And what about Kate?'

'Kate wants them, too. It's all part of what happens when there's a mutual look.'

'How is the valley?' Jane broke in a little frantically; she found she wanted to hold something off until she caught her breath, as it were. She needed time.

'It will recover. Australian fires clean up, but rarely destroy.'

'And John's place?'

'Untouched. He and his Ennie defended it successfully, they'll be a great team.' As before, William said: 'I'm sorry, Jane,' and she knew he meant John.

'It's all right.' Jane repeated her reply.

'Then it appears I'm quite clear,' William said matter-of-factly. 'No use you bringing out Tim, he and Maureen practically have announced their engagement.'

'At no time had I any intention of bringing out Tim, as you put it, and I'm happy about them.' Jane stopped and looked at William. 'What do you mean you're clear?' she demanded.

188

'To put it to you.'

'Put what?' Jane stared incredulously at him.

'I want us to be married. Frankly I wanted that the first moment I saw you making a mess of your shipboard strapper chores.'

'I didn't!'

'You tethered them the wrong way, remember? But' ... a pause ... 'you knew how to tether my heart. I knew who you were, and I was determined to dislike you. You'd let Gair down.'

'I hadn't!'

'I know that now. In a way I knew it then. Rodden Gair was clever, but never an intrinsic character. However, in black and white it sounded as though you'd taken him up the garden path. I had to go on facts, Jane.'

'Where is Rodden now?'

'Oh, I haven't victimized him, in fact quite the opposite. I've secured him a very good city job, where he'll undoubtedly go right to the top by marrying the boss's daughter.'

'He only looked on the commercial side,' Jane murmured, 'naturally I thought it was his boss's way, too.'

'And you still don't know, do you? You know nothing about your boss's ways, nor' ... an oblique look ... 'your boss.'

'Co-director,' Jane corrected.

'Of four-fifths. You have only one-fifth. Jane, *Jane*, one-fifth of what?'

'Of Gretel, San Marco, Ruthven, of—Mr. Bower! William! William, what on earth——'

For William Bower had lifted her right out of the bed into his arms, she was in those arms tightly, so tightly that unless she struggled very effectively she would never break loose.

'One-fifth will do, Jane,' William Bower was saying. 'I would sooner you met me halfway, but I've enough for the whole way, and if you find you can't contribute——'

'Contribute what?'

'What it takes to make two. You see, girl, I love you. It

only took one look.'

'But a mutual look,' Jane said quietly, unprepared for the almost violent manner he now put her on her feet.

'Don't say that if you don't mean it, Jane.' William held her at arm's length.

'And if I do mean it, William?'

'Then say it. Say it.'

'What I have is five-fifths,' she told him. 'That makes the whole, doesn't it, William?'

'And the look?' he reminded her jealously.

'A mutual one. I said so. Oh, William' ... up in his big arms again ... 'everything is so perfect, so very perfect, yet Dandy...'

'Yes, Dandy. But it was to be, my sweet. Try to accept that.'

She did accept it, though sadly, her head against his shoulder, his fingers tight on the flimsy stuff of the nightgown in which Teresa must have encased her. In a bitter sweetness she heard him say, 'Oh, there was a cable from my uncle for you. Evidently he must have left out something in his answer regarding Dotsy.'

'Dotsy's condition, when, but not by whom,' Jane murmured.

'Yes, darling.' He handed her the envelope and she opened it up.

She was crying and smiling as she looked up again from the message, crying because something was over, smiling because something would soon begin. A little shaky foal would begin, a fragment of wet ears, soft eyes and bewildered expression. Dotsy's foal.

And ... handing William the cable ... *Dandy's* doing. For that was what was written.

MISS SIDNEY STOP BOWERS STUD STOP PLATEAU STOP IT WAS DANDY STOP

Then there was signed: RUSTY.

All this, knew Jane in William's arms, and *still* Dandy.

have you heard about Harlequin's great new series?

Harlequin Presents

* ANNE HAMPSON
* ANNE MATHER
* VIOLET WINSPEAR

These three very popular Harlequin authors have written many outstanding romances which we have not been able to include in the regular Harlequin series.

Now we have made special arrangements to publish many of these delightful never — before — available stories in a new author series, called "Harlequin Presents".

See reverse of page for complete listing of titles available.

Harlequin Presents..

Three of the world's greatest romance authors.
Don't miss any of this new series. Only 75c each!

ANNE HAMPSON

- [ ] #1 GATES OF STEEL
- [ ] #2 MASTER OF MOONROCK
- [ ] #7 DEAR STRANGER
- [ ] #10 WAVES OF FIRE
- [ ] #13 A KISS FROM SATAN
- [ ] #16 WINGS OF NIGHT
- [ ] #19 SOUTH OF MANDRAKI
- [ ] #22 THE HAWK AND THE DOVE
- [ ] #25 BY FOUNTAINS WILD
- [ ] #28 DARK AVENGER

ANNE MATHER

- [ ] #3 SWEET REVENGE
- [ ] #4 THE PLEASURE & THE PAIN
- [ ] #8 THE SANCHEZ TRADITION
- [ ] #11 WHO RIDES THE TIGER
- [ ] #14 STORM IN A RAIN BARREL
- [ ] #17 LIVING WITH ADAM
- [ ] #20 A DISTANT SOUND OF THUNDER
- [ ] #23 THE LEGEND OF LEXANDROS
- [ ] #26 DARK ENEMY
- [ ] #29 MONKSHOOD

VIOLET WINSPEAR

- [ ] #5 DEVIL IN A SILVER ROOM
- [ ] #6 THE HONEY IS BITTER
- [ ] #9 WIFE WITHOUT KISSES
- [ ] #12 DRAGON BAY
- [ ] #15 THE LITTLE NOBODY
- [ ] #18 THE KISSES AND THE WINE
- [ ] #21 THE UNWILLING BRIDE
- [ ] #24 PILGRIM'S CASTLE
- [ ] #27 HOUSE OF STRANGERS
- [ ] #30 BRIDE OF LUCIFER

To: HARLEQUIN READER SERVICE, Dept. N 312

M.P.O. Box 707, Niagara Falls, N.Y. 14302

Canadian address: Stratford, Ont., Canada

- [ ] Please send me the free Harlequin Romance Presents Catalogue.

- [ ] Please send me the titles checked.

I enclose $_____ (No C.O.D.'s). All books are 75c each. To help defray postage and handling cost, please add 25c.

Name _____

Address _____

City/Town _____

State/Prov. _____ Zip _____

N 312